SNOW & MISTLETOE

This is a work of fiction. Names, characters, organizations, places, events, and incidents are either products of the author's imagination, or are used fictitiously.

Text Copyright © 2019 Rie Anders

"You're what?"

The words, 'We're going to have to let you go,' hung in the air between us. I stared across the pretentious, gaudy mahogany desk at my boss, who was—at this moment in time—firing me. Well, he wasn't so much firing me as laying me off. Regardless, the outcome was the same: I no longer had a job.

"I'm sorry, Caitlyn." He always called me by my formal name. My name is Caitlyn Darling, but I have gone by Cat for as long as I can remember. It took me a long time to realize my last name was actually Darling. I'd always thought my teachers were calling me, "Cat, darling."

My boss's mouth was still moving, and I refocused my attention on him. "The revenues for this year just won't sustain additional staff next year, and we

3

thought it would be best to give you notice before the holidays."

His fat, ruddy face was blurring in front of me, and I focused on Elliott Bay out the window behind him so that I could clear my vision. The clear blue sky was reflected in the bay below, and gave the illusion that it was much warmer than today's 37-degree temperature. The weather forecasters had said snow for Christmas, but current conditions didn't make that seem likely. Weren't they wrong most of the time anyway?

He continued, "You can leave today, and we'll pay you through the end of the year."

I thought to myself, *Maybe if you sold this ugly desk and your Cadillac Escalade, you could keep me for another year.*

Taking a deep breath, I wrung my fingers together, and tried not to cry. Working in advertising had been my dream job right out of college. *Starling Design's* clients included Patagonia, K2, Sherpa Adventure Gear, and a number of other outdoor companies in Seattle. Helping them shape their image gave me a great deal of satisfaction. I loved knowing that my designs could inspire the public to purchase their products, and be a part of the outdoor lifestyle they were selling.

My graduation had been postponed a year because I'd interspersed my academic semesters with internships. My parents had wanted me to get a "respectable" degree, but I had never wanted to do anything other than graphic design. We didn't have much money growing up, and they were worried I would always be poor. We lived east of Seattle in a really small town called North Bend. My mom worked at the public library, and my dad was an art teacher.

I, apparently, believed in myself a little more than they did, and started entering my work in design contests and graphic arts competitions. I eventually caught the eye of K2 skis, and they hired me to freelance on a winter campaign.

The campaign didn't pay me very much, but it was enough to boost my confidence in my talent, and I applied to Cornish College of the Arts and was accepted. Tuition was incredibly expensive, so I applied for financial aid and scholarships, freelancing and submitting my work to contests in my spare time. All of my hard work paid off when I was hired at *Starling Design*, where I've been since I graduated six years ago.

I'd never been let go before, and I felt sick to my stomach. "Mr. Peterson, I'm unclear about how this works. Is there someone in HR who can help me?"

He slid a packet over to me, nodded, and said, "Your final paycheck and 6 weeks' severance are in there. One week for every year you've been with us. You have a week to submit the acknowledgment forms and sign up for medical insurance. You will need to leave your key card, badge, and computer with security on your way out today." His chin was folding over the neck of his shirt, and I briefly wondered if he could breathe. I also couldn't understand how he had risen to Vice President of the creative design team when he clearly knew nothing about art.

It was 3 o'clock on the Friday afternoon before the Christmas holidays. I was leaving Monday morning to go skiing in Aspen with my boyfriend, Sam, and now all I could think about was that I needed to find a new job. Sam was going to flip out. I was going to flip out.

"Do I have time to clean out my desk?" I sat primly in front of him. My 4-inch stilettos were tapping furiously on the plush carpet of his office, and I was grateful he couldn't hear them. Tap, tap, tap—my leg bounced frantically.

He leaned across the table, and I saw sweat beading on his forehead. Was he going to have a heart attack? *Please, dear God. Please let him have a heart attack so I can keep my job.*

I wasn't that fortunate.

"Your accounts have already been transferred over to Paul Hanley. You're free to clean out your desk now and leave." He shuffled some papers around on his desk, and then looked in a drawer, seemingly uncomfortable that I was still sitting here.

What the heck? Paul Hanley, that doofus? My self-esteem just fell through the floor. Paul was a junior design artist and had only been with the company since June. Little levers in my head started clicking like dominoes, and I suddenly remembered that Paul was the owner's nephew.

It was time to put my big girl panties on, hold my head high, and walk out of this shithole of an office. I couldn't argue. I couldn't even think straight, and even if I could, nothing was going to change the outcome.

I stood to my full 5 feet 9 inches (well, 5'5 without shoes), and gathered up the papers from his desk. Tears were brimming in my eyes, and I fought to keep them from falling in front of him.

"I assume that you will give me a good reference?" It was taking all my gumption not to pick up the stapler off his desk and throw it at his head.

"Of course. Of course. Everything you need to know is in your packet. Phone numbers for employment verification and unemployment—everything."

Ouch! Unemployment. I hadn't even gotten that far in my thinking. He was ten steps ahead of me.

"Right. Unemployment. Of course." A tear fell from my eyes to the packet in my arms, and I knew I needed to escape. Fast. Before I had a complete meltdown.

I reached across the desk to shake his hand, and he heaved himself halfway out of his chair to return the gesture.

"Thank you for the generous severance, and I hope you have a merry Christmas and a happy New Year." I added in my head, *You, bad Santa.*

Calmly—but with purpose—I went to the door, left his office, and shut the door quietly behind me. Continuing down the hall to the elevators, I waited for the one that would take me back down to my floor and eventually out the front door.

When it arrived, I stepped in with a few members of the accounting team.

"Hey, guys, leaving for the holidays?" I pasted a smile on my face.

Nerdy Steve responded, "We're headed to the Owl and Thistle for a few drinks, if you want to join us."

"Oh, thanks, but I have a lot to do before the holidays. I'm going to have to pass, but you guys have fun. I love that place."

One of the other accountants asked me if I had plans for Christmas. Saved by the bell, the elevator stopped at my floor, and I stepped out.

When the elevator doors shut behind me, I stopped in the middle of the hall and sent a quick text to Sam.

Sam, please call me

Placing my phone back on the top of the packet, I quickly went to my office to gather my things. The offices were all quiet, since most of the designers had already left for the weekend. As I came around the corner, I noticed a crate of boxes and a security guard ready to help me. He saw me, and I stopped in my tracks, put one finger up to indicate "one minute," and turned back towards the bathrooms.

As soon as I entered the bathroom, I locked myself in a stall and started to cry. At first it was just the silent kind: the one that digs deep into the pain, but doesn't make any noise until you hit the point of no return. Then I sobbed. The tears fell from my eyes, and I crossed my arms in front of me in a hug. This was unbelievable.

When my tears subsided, I took some deep breaths and tried to call Sam. It went to voicemail, so I hung up and exited the bathroom stall.

The guard was still at my office door when I returned, and I greeted him with a smile. "You must be here to walk me out?"

"Yes, ma'am," he responded coldly without a smile. *Ma'am?* Maybe he can remove the knife he just verbally shoved in my heart.

"Right. Okay." I smiled a closed-lip smile at him and took one of the boxes from the stack. I stood in the middle of my office and just looked around. There wasn't anything I wanted except a few pictures of me with my family, and one of me and Sam taken at Cannon Beach last spring.

I took my Longchamp tote out of my overhead and stuffed my pictures in the bag. "I'm ready."

Walking in front of him, I kept my head up, and prayed I wouldn't see anyone I knew. They would all know soon enough. And I wasn't fired, so there was that. At least, I kept reminding myself I wasn't fired, just let go. It became a mantra in my head.

When we reached the glass front doors of the building, I turned to the guard and handed him my badge, which also acted as my computer key. He took it from me unsmilingly, and walked away. I stared after him in disbelief. This was so surreal.

I exited the front door and walked across the street to the parking garage. I quickly located my Fiat Spider convertible and settled in for the drive...where? Home? I guess. When I buckled in, I texted Sam again: *I've had a crappy day, please take me to dinner tonight...why aren't you answering me?*

Staring out the windshield of my car, I saw on the dashboard that it was only three-thirty. The last thirty minutes had felt like a lifetime. Sam and I usually had plans on Fridays, but maybe he was working late to get ready for our trip.

Every year for Christmas, he and his family rented a house in Aspen, and this year, he'd asked me to go with him. Christmas was my favorite holiday. I wanted to be with my family, but this year, my younger sister and her husband were in San Francisco with a new baby and didn't want to travel. It was a perfect Christmas to go skiing with Sam and his family.

Sam and I met on a Saturday evening wine cruise almost two years ago. My last roommate was getting married, and she wanted a wine cruise to be her bachelorette party.

When I'd started at Cornish, I'd rented a room in a house on Queen Anne with two other girls, Shaye Richards and Erin McAllister. Shaye was a quiet girl, and kept to herself, but Erin and I were always out at the clubs and local bars. Shaye bought her own house a few years after we all graduated, and we rented her room to Susan Gray.

Susan was the one getting married. And ironically, she was marrying Ned Fox, so she would be Susan Gray Fox.

The night of the party, all the girls had met at our house. A party bus limo had picked us all up there, and I had planned to call Uber for anyone who needed a ride home after the event.

When we arrived at the dock for the two-hour cruise, I saw Sam immediately. He was a golden boy across a sea of Seattle grunge. I tripped getting out of the bus, and he grabbed me as my heel caught on the curb.

"Easy, there—you ok?" I could have sworn I saw a sparkle on his tooth.

"I'm fine, yes, thank you." I stuttered a bit before brushing imaginary lint off of my black cocktail dress.

"You girls going on the wine cruise tonight?" I bristled at his use of the word "girls," but ignored it and beamed up at him.

"Yes, my friend Susan is getting married next weekend. This is her bachelorette party, of sorts." The girls were still unloading off of the bus, and wandering towards the ticketing booth where we would board the small 200-passenger cruise ship for the evening.

"And you?" I stood next to him as others joined him.

"No, I'm not getting married next weekend."

Blushing, I started to say, 'You know what I mean,' but then I looked into his sparkling blue eyes and saw that he was laughing at me.

He saved me by adding, "I'm entertaining some clients tonight, and I thought this would be a cool Seattle event to share with them."

I was so overwhelmed by his charm, I lost track of all the girls from the bus. Frantically looking around for them, biting my lower lip in confusion, I said, "I seem to have lost my friends."

He saw my discomfort and said, "Come on, join us. We'll find them."

I ended up spending most of the evening with him, and when the boat returned to the dock after cruising around Elliott Bay, he asked for my number.

He called me the next day, and we've been together ever since.

Except for now, when he wouldn't answer his phone.

I texted him one more time before I drove out of the garage.

Sam, I'm headed home. See you there?

I drove up First Avenue towards Queen Anne hill, to the three-bedroom house I rented with Erin. It was just the two of us now, since Susan had moved out. We liked the quiet, and since we were making more money than we had in the past, we didn't need a third person to share the rent. We had turned the third bedroom into an office and workout room, and I would use both when I got home.

Parking my car on the back street behind the house, I went down the steps that led into our backyard, and through the back door into the kitchen. The kitchen led into the dining room on the left, which circled into the living room, which had a picture window that looked out over Lake Union. The living room led around to the front foyer, where a grand staircase went upstairs to the three bedrooms and one bathroom.

The stairs creaked like those in old houses do, but other than that, the house was quiet. Erin was probably still at work.

My room was in the back, looking towards the back yard. I changed into yoga pants and a bra-tank, and then I checked my phone. Nothing from Sam. Starting to get worried, and a little frustrated, I called his office before I went to the office/pseudo-workout-room.

"Global Marine Insurance, this is Jeanette. How may I help you?" Sam's secretary answered, and I was so relieved to hear her voice, I audibly sighed.

"Jeanette, it's Cat, is Sam there?"

Her voice was clipped and panicky when she responded. "Oh, hi, Cat. Uh, no. He left already."

Cradling the phone against my ear, I went into the office and sat down at my desk.

"Okay, well, I've been trying to reach him, and he's not responding. If he checks in, would you please let him know I called?"

"I sure will. You have a good holiday. Good-bye."

Holding my phone away from me, I stared at it in shock, surprised at her clipped hang-up.

I set my phone next to my computer and logged on, waiting for my email to come up. The very first one was from Sam.

To: Cat Darling
From: Sam Stevens
Subject: I'm sorry

Cat,

I'm sorry I'm doing this via email. There just never seemed to be a good time or a good place to do this.

For the past few months, I have been seeing someone else, and we have grown very close. I'm taking her to Aspen, and I'm ending my relationship with you.

I wish you the very best in life, and I'm so grateful to have shared such a wonderful time with you.

Merry Christmas,
Sam

"What. The. Fuck."

"What?" Erin was sitting cross-legged on the couch, and I was curled up in a ball crying.

I couldn't even see through my tears, and my eyes were starting to puff up. Preparation H was going to be my friend tonight.

"I don't understand, either." I hiccupped, and continued, "I thought everything was fine. We hadn't seen each other in a while because he was traveling so much, but I was really excited for our trip to Aspen. And now he's taking someone else, and he broke up with meeeeeee." I sobbed all over again and buried my face in the pillow.

Erin was rubbing my back, trying to calm my tears.

After a few more minutes, she shook my shoulder and said, "Okay, you need to stop. We can't just sit around here and have you feeling sorry for yourself. We're going out."

"You're joking, right?" I reached for a Kleenex from the box on the coffee table and blew my nose.

"No, I'm absolutely not joking. You can feel sorry for yourself all weekend long, cry, eat ice cream, sleep, whatever." She stood and flailed her arms above her head. "But tonight, we're going out, and you can think about this mess on Monday."

"When I wake up, jobless, and my boyfriend is skiing in Aspen without me?" Head back against the cushions, I stuck my feet straight out in front of me, lounged back on the couch, and looked up at her.

Laughing at me, she said, "You look pathetic. Get up." Reaching for my hand, she heaved me up off the couch. "Go shower. Get sexy. I'll find a place for us to have dinner, and then its downtown, baby." She walked off to the kitchen wiggling her hips.

I trudged up the stairs to my room and went directly to my small walk-in closet to find something to wear. My queen-sized bed was calling to me: the purple duvet, fluffy and inviting, beckoned to me to crawl under it. I resisted the urge, and grabbed a sequined mini-skirt with flapper fringe down to my knees, and a plain black tank. Black strappy sandals, and a black fake-fur shrug completed my look. I would only freeze when we were outside, right?

Laying the clothes out on my bed, I went to the bathroom to take a long hot shower. Hoping to wash away the miserable day, I stayed under the spray, eyes closed, head against the glass, until my fingers started to shrivel.

A rap on the door brought me back from my musings of the horrible turn of events today. "Hurry up! I need a shower too."

"Give me five minutes."

"How does Metropolitan Grill sound for dinner? And then dancing downtown after?" She yelled through the door.

I shouted back at her, above the sound of the water, "Sounds perfect."

Back in my room, I took my time getting ready. I blew out my dark shoulder-length hair, and applied way too much eyeliner and red lipstick. At this point, I didn't care. My boobs were beautiful and voluptuous, and I was going full-on tart tonight, so I wore a push-up bra so that they rose out of my tank top.

My mom's voice was clear in my head with a phrase she would always say when I was a teenager: 'Put some lipstick on, and get out of the house, Cat. Something has to happen.'

Ok, Mom, taking your advice tonight.

I met Erin downstairs. She was dressed in black leather pants, a gold sequin halter top, and big hoop earrings. We were certainly sparkly tonight.

"Ready?" She had flat-ironed her long red hair, and she looked like an Irish girl right out of the seventies.

Inhaling deeply, I puffed out my cheeks as I exhaled and said, "I guess."

We took an Uber for the ten-minute ride downtown, and he dropped us off in front of the restaurant.

"You girls be safe tonight. Looking good."

Erin was already out of the car, so she didn't hear him. I paused a moment to look at him, his leery face a little clearer now that he had spoken directly to me, and I found his attention a little creepy. "Uh, thanks. Have a good night."

Stepping out of the car, I shut the door behind me, and we entered the restaurant. The windows had fake snow blown on them, and the inside of the restaurant was decorated with tinsel and lights. Gold garland and large gold balls hung from the chandeliers, creating a festive atmosphere.

The chatter of the bar greeted me, and I felt a spark of energy. Maybe Erin had the right idea. Maybe this would be fun. Dark cherry wood made the restaurant feel classy, giving it an air of distinction, and the brass railings shined from attentive polishing. Just behind the hostess stand stood a 12-foot Christmas tree, wrapped in blue and silver ribbon and decorated in hand blown glass fishes and ferry boats.

As the hostess walked us to a booth, I glanced at the crowd in the bar and felt a pang of envy for what appeared to be their perfect little worlds. I hoped the crushing emotions of losing my job and my boyfriend in the same day were not too close to the surface, and that I could enjoy myself tonight.

We were seated at a booth with plush, green velvet cushions, and I sunk into it and tried to adjust my skirt.

"I think..." I started to laugh. "I think I'm going to have difficulty in this skirt tonight. These velvet seats are not easy to slide across."

"Try to sit closer to the edge so that you don't look awkward." Erin smiled at me and picked up the wine list.

The table was meticulously set, with the napkin in the center of our place settings folded like a fan. A small flower arrangement and votive candle completed the sophisticated look.

"Thank you for getting me out of the house tonight. Now that I've had time to think about it, it was kind of a shitty thing for him to do. And I didn't deserve that."

"Uh, *yeah*!" She spoke vehemently, and I was surprised at the level of contempt in her voice.

"Did you not like him?"

"Oh, sweetie, he was so basic. You are so not."

"Seriously? All this time? Why didn't you say anything?" I was shocked and a little hurt.

"It wasn't my place. Besides, I knew you would figure it out eventually."

I felt my shoulders drop, and I lowered my head.

She spoke sternly to me. "Get your head up. Stick out those boobs." I snapped my head up and looked at her with wide eyes. "Do not be embarrassed or let him shame you. You're a hot little beauty, and you're too good for him. You have been pulled together, focused, and checking all the right boxes. Don't let this one event set you back. Now, it's time for you to look around at what you're missing." She swung her arm towards the bar, as if displaying a prize, and I saw it differently from when we had walked in. I saw attractive men in suits, smiling and joking. Hot men, not vanilla blonds.

Grinning and looking at her sideways, I said cheekily, "I could just have fun tonight."

"And every night, my friend. Now where is our waitress?"

We ordered almond crusted scallops to start, with a bottle of white wine, and we both had filet mignon for dinner. The steak was prepared perfectly, and melted in my mouth.

"Mmmmmmm. This is so good!" I cut another small piece, placed the morsel in my mouth, and closed my eyes to savor the moment.

I was disrupted by a voice at the side of our table. "Ladies, good evening. I'm Walt, and this is my friend Perry."

Erin introduced us while I finished chewing.

Swallowing my dinner, I took a sip of my wine and said hello.

"We noticed you were having a nice dinner and wanted to invite you to join us at the bar when you're finished." He was average height, blond hair, brown eyes, and attractive. He was also very polite, and we were on a mission to have fun tonight, so why not.

I looked at Erin for subtle confirmation and when I saw her covert nod, I responded. "We'd like that very much, thank you."

His friend was a little quieter, and was eyeing Erin with appreciation. She was smiling up at him, and if I had any doubt that she was interested, it disappeared when I saw her smirk, and tilt her head.

Raising his glass to me, Perry glanced at Erin, and then the two men went back to the bar.

"Merry Christmas to me," she said in a sing-song tone.

"Yes, but we stick together. We dance together. We go home together. Got it?"

"Got it!" She looked stern, and I laughed at her.

Finishing our dinner, we paid our bill and went into the bar to join Walt and Perry. The bar was louder now that the hour had gotten later, and people were relaxing.

Walt ordered a round of Fireball whiskey, and toasted to a merry Christmas.

I pasted a smile on my face that was both a grimace and a grin, and said, "To a Merry Christmas."

Raising the glass to my mouth, I shot the whiskey back, shook my body from the cinnamon heat, and let out an "Ack."

The guys laughed, and Walt waved at the bartender for another round.

"Uh, let's wait a minute until I catch up."

A customer next to us vacated a stool, and I jumped up on it, and crossed my legs.

Perry joined the conversation, and asked us what the occasion was for our night out.

Erin drawled, "Well, Cat here just got a promotion at work. Aaaaaaaand she is flying to Cancun tomorrow with her boyfriend for Christmas. So, we are celebrating her amazing day!"

Bless her heart! She was my greatest cheerleader right now, and my heart just about burst.

"Wow! That is fantastic! Congratulations! On both parts." Walt looked a little disappointed, but I was quite certain he would not be lonely for long. His confidence and Peter Facinelli looks, from a purely objective standpoint, were very attractive. Ironically, I'd always been attracted to blonds, but now he just reminded me of Sam.

"Thank you, I'm very excited." I glanced at Erin, and she was smirking at me, laughing that I was playing along.

Perry saved me from explaining the details and mentioned they were headed down to Aston Manor. "A friend of ours works as a bouncer, and we can bring you two in with us, if you like."

He was looking at me, for permission, and glancing back at Erin as if to say, 'I know you're out with your friend, but please, please, please convince her, so that I can hang out with you.'

Nodding my agreement, I said, "I think that sounds like a great plan!" Erin put her hands together prayer-position in front of her chest, and mouthed "thank you," which prompted Perry to reach out and grab her in a hug.

We had another round of drinks, and then Walt pulled out his phone and called up an Uber.

The bar was filling up with couples on dates, and singles out for the night, as we grabbed our coats and went outside to wait for our ride. Aston Manor was just a short distance from the restaurant, and the streets were lined with holiday decorations: wreaths hanging from lamp-posts, and windows decorated with garland. I felt a pang of sadness that Christmas was just a few days away, and

I appeared to be spending it alone. There wasn't time for me to get a flight to San Francisco, and Erin was going to Bellingham to be with her family. I shook my head and refocused on having fun. I would figure it out tomorrow.

A line was starting to form around the side of the building when we arrived, but Walt walked right up to the bouncer, shook his hand, and gave him a man hug as he slapped him on the back.

"Got room for us and the girls tonight?" he asked the bouncer.

I tried not to roll my eyes at his demeaning tone, and just smiled at the bouncer.

His neck was so big it looked like it could swallow his head, and his shoulders seemed immovable. He gave us an appreciative look, and then reached down and unlatched the red velour rope. The doors opened, and the electronic beat of the music drew me toward the dance floor. We weaved our way through the crowd, Erin bouncing around behind me.

I stopped at the coat check and gave the vapid-looking girl my shrug. She handed me a numbered ticket, and I put it in my wristlet as we worked our way to the bar.

The club was the size of a warehouse, with an open dance floor and a second story that wrapped around the edges like a catwalk. Purple, pink, blue, and yellow strobe lights pulsed to the music, and a huge chandelier in an iconic 1920s style hung in the middle of the room.

After another round of shots, I saw an acrobat hanging from the ceiling. Glitter flew off of her as she spun around a rope.

Erin and Perry were now wrapped around each other, and I tried to stick close, without interrupting their moment. Walt was looking distracted, and I couldn't blame him. We had essentially warned him away from me.

"Walt, get us another round and let's dance," I shouted over the music, and he perked up.

We did another shot, and I yanked on his arm to pull him out on the dance floor. A dark-haired girl in a sequined tank dress came around with vials of tequila, and Walt bought us two.

"Look, we match!" I smiled at her, bobbing my head, and pointing to my skirt. Her face remained passive as she paused for a moment to look at me and gave Walt back his card. "The sequins? We match."

She turned and walked away from me, and I just started to laugh.

Walt and I danced, together, but a bit in our own little worlds. All the songs merged into one another, and I lost track of time. The lady in the tank dress returned a few times, and Walt just kept buying tequila for us.

My hair was sticking to my neck from sweat, and I felt free. Out of the corner of my eye, I saw a red silk rope with a hula hoop connected to it lowering beside me. A very large-chested woman in a black bustier was suddenly beside me, holding out the hoop for me to get on.

I shouted above the music, "Seriously?"

She nodded, and held the hoop while I sat on it. She lifted herself back above the hoop to the silk rope and lifted her legs in a split as we started to rise from the ground.

The music was resonating in my chest, and I could feel my ribs rattling as we started to spin above the crowd.

Looking down, I saw Erin break from Perry, and she followed underneath me. I saw Walt yanking on her arm, and after that, things got a little fuzzy.

I was being lowered back down over the bar, and when my feet touched down, I started dancing. My hair flying around me, I pulled my phone out of my wristlet and started taking selfies.

Erin was beneath me, making sure I was ok, and I noticed that Walt had disappeared.

The alcohol and the techno beat were putting me in a trance, and somewhere near me I smelled Viktor and Rolf Flowerbomb. The sweet, flowery smell that I usually found so girly made me a bit nauseous.

I looked down at Erin and said, "I think I'm going to be sick!"

"What?!" she shouted up at me.

My legs started to wobble, and I lowered myself down onto the bar. I kind of just wanted to lay there, but the bartender shoved at my bottom to help push me over the edge.

I landed on unstable footing and fell into Erin. "I think I'm going to be sick," I slurred, and felt myself folding over.

Erin grabbed my elbow and walked me to the door, stopping to get my shrug on the way out. Leaning against the wall, I waited for her, and then she took me outside. Inhaling the cold, winter air, I walked with her around the back side of the building.

Stopping alongside the alley, I leaned over and got sick all over the street, while Erin held my hair back.

I heard Erin chuckle, and when I felt I didn't have anything left in me, I stood.

"Well, it's official. I hate myself."

3

"Hey, Cardi B, I brought you some aspirin."

Erin was standing next to my bed, with a glass of water in one hand and two aspirin in the other.

I slowly peeled my eyelids open, caked makeup making it difficult, and saw that she was dressed for a run.

I started to speak. "Did I..."

My voice was hoarse, so I sat up, took the water from her, and drank down the aspirin.

Lying back down, I closed my eyes and tried again. "Did I leave my dignity at the bar?"

Erin laughed and said, "Oh, darlin', not only that, but you left your self-respect, your sense of decency, all manners of grace, and quite possibly, I think, your underwear."

I groaned and put my forearm over my eyes. She sat down on the mattress, and I scooted over a bit to make room for her.

"And now, my beautiful friend, you can grieve." She reached out and took my arm off my face.

Opening my eyes, I saw that hers looked sad, and her smile consoling.

Tearing up, I said, "Will you bring me some coffee?"

"Of course I will, and then I'm going for a run and breakfast with Perry."

I turned to my side. "Well, that worked out well for you, didn't it?"

She shrugged. "He was nice. I liked him."

Holding back my tears, I said, "Have fun. I'll just be here, dying from a number of shameful adjectives."

Laughing at me, she stood and said, "You'll be fine in a few weeks, I promise." She left my room to get me some coffee.

Sniffling, I reached for my phone and saw that I had ten missed messages. Dialing my voicemail, I listened to them one after the other. Dear Lord, what had I done?

The first three were from my mom. I'd called her before we went out last night and left a message about Sam and my job. I hadn't called her back after that, and she was worried about me.

The next one was from Sam, and I sat up to listen.

Cat, please don't call me again. I'm sorry we ended the way we did, but you cannot call and scream at me. Quite frankly, your tone scared me, and I don't think your choice of words was warranted.

Oh my God! What did I do?

Erin came back in with my coffee, and I looked at her, eyes wide with panic. She stopped short at my door. "What happened?"

"I think I called Sam last night. I don't remember, but he left me a message never to call him again. I'm so embarrassed."

She placed my coffee on the nightstand, and I played the message for her.

"Oh, goodness!" She crossed her arms in front of her.

I dropped my head in my hands and started to cry.

"Sweetie, I'm so sorry." She was rubbing my back. "What else is on the phone?"

"A few messages from my mom, and a couple of others."

"Let's listen to them. Let's rip the Band-Aid off so you can move on."

I dialed up my voicemail again and we listened to the next messages.

*Hey, Cat, this is Tom, you were smokin' hot last and...*Delete.

Erin covered her mouth to hold back her laugh. Her eyes were crinkling.

Cat, this is Walt. Just wanted to make sure you girls got home ok. I kind of lost you last night and was a little worried about you. Call me back.

"Huh. That was nice."

*Hey, babe, Jack here...*Delete. I raised my phone, and shook it. "What the heck? Why weren't you keeping track of me?"

"I was!" she exclaimed. "I couldn't pin you down and keep you off your phone, though."

Hey Sis, Mom's worried about you. Do you want to come to San Francisco for

38

the holidays? It's not too late to drive. Call me.

"My brother," I said longingly.

Cat, this is Shaye. I looked sharply at Erin, eyebrows raised. *Are you ok? I got a message from you that was garbled, and it sounded like you were crying. I hope you're doing all right. It was nice to hear your voice again, even if you sounded distraught. We're around this morning, but we're flying out later today to Hawaii for the holidays. Call me back. Hope you're ok.*

"That was interesting. I wonder what I told her." I stared pensively out the window in front of me.

"Call her back. I need to go. I'll be back later today, and then I'm going to my parents' tomorrow."

"Ok. I'll be here."

She paused one last time to look at me, and I said, "Go! I'm fine."

Staring at my phone, I contemplated calling Shaye. I hadn't seen her in years. The last I knew, she had married a guy she knew from her childhood, and they had a couple of kids.

She had always been very private and worked a lot when we lived together. Not anti-social, just reserved.

Apprehension filled me about calling her back. I don't really know why I called her in the first place. I flipped the phone over and over in my palm for a few minutes before tapping in her number on the keypad, calling her back.

She answered after a few rings, "This is Shaye."

"Shaye, its Caitlyn," I greeted her.

"Cat, how are you? Are you ok?"

"I'm fine. I'm so sorry I worried you. I had...I had a bad day yesterday. I lost my job and my boyfriend broke up with me, so I was kind of a train wreck. Erin and I went out last night, and I had too much to drink. I'm so sorry I called you."

"Oh, Cat. That's awful. How awful for you."

"Yeah. Sam, my boyfriend, and I were supposed to be going to Aspen for the holidays, and now, well—now he's with someone else, and my parents are in San Francisco. I think I'm feeling a little sorry for myself. I don't even remember calling you, but you must have been on my mind if I called you crying."

"I've missed you. We haven't talked in a few years. I'm glad you still have my number."

"Me too. You said you're going to Hawaii for Christmas? That sounds fun."

"Yeah, we bought a townhouse in Lahaina and wanted to spend Christmas there this year. You know what? I just realized the cabin will be empty this year. We usually rent it out, but we wanted to do some remodeling, so we took it off the website. Nick already lent our house out to a friend of his, but you could stay in the cabin if you wanted to."

"Shaye, I couldn't do that."

"Nonsense. The more I think about it, the more I feel it's the right thing. Your parents are away, and maybe it'll be good for you to process this away from home. What do you say?"

"Well..."

"Say yes, Cat. It'll be good for you."

"Are you sure?"

"I'm positive. Listen, JT is throwing himself on the floor, and I need to finish packing. I'll send you an email from the car with instructions, and there's a six o'clock ferry you could be on tonight if you wanted."

"Thank you, Shaye. Thank you"

"You're welcome. And next time, let's have a longer conversation."

She hung up on me, and I sat staring at my phone.

Despite the clammy feeling on my skin, my serious dehydration, the bags under my eyes, and the cotton balls I felt like I had in my mouth, I was excited about getting out of town.

Tossing aside the covers, I put my feet to the floor, got my bearings, and headed to the shower.

The hot spray beat down on my head and back, and I started to feel a little better, somewhat human, and much more awake.

My coconut lime body wash invigorated me, and when I finally felt like my eyes were free of makeup, I turned the water off, stepped out, and wrapped myself in a large fluffy towel.

I towel dried my hair and wrapped it in a smaller towel, traded my body towel for the green bathrobe on the back of the door, and went downstairs to make some greasy bacon and eggs.

Our kitchen was bright and airy, with twelve-foot-high ceilings. The house was built in 1912, and it had that musty old smell so common in older homes in the Pacific Northwest.

I pulled the toaster out from under the counter and the bread from the bread box, craving carbs to go along with my greasy bacon.

While the bacon was sizzling on the stove, I cracked two eggs, added some salt and pepper, a little bit of cheese, and some milk to make them fluffy, scrambling them in the pan next to the bacon.

When my breakfast was finished cooking, I sat down at the dining room table with another cup of coffee, and called my mom while I ate.

She answered on the third ring. "Cat! What on Earth, sweetie? What took you so long to call? And are you alright? You need to get down here and spend Christmas with us. Your brother has plenty of room, and we would love to have you with us. You know we were so sad that you were going to Aspen in the first place. Now. Do you need help with a plane ticket? When can you come?"

"Hi, Mom."

"Hi, honey. Sorry, I'm just so worried about you, and so angry at that little shit, Sam."

"Mom! I'm fine. I'm going to be ok."

"I'm sure you are, sweetie, but you need to be with us now. Your father is looking at flights, and you can come to San Francisco."

"Actually, Mom, I think I'm going to the San Juan's for a week over Christmas. Do you remember my former roommate, Shaye?"

"The tall quiet blonde?"

"Yes."

"Kind of. Nice girl? Kept to herself?"

"Yes, that's her. Well, I talked to her this morning, and she and her family are going to Hawaii for the week, and she said I could stay in their cabin."

"Oh, honey, why would you want to be alone?"

"Honestly, Mom, I'm kind of reeling from the past twenty-four hours, and being alone in the woods to clear my head and think about what I'm doing next sounds like   exactly what I need."

"But I hate to think of you alone on Christmas."

"I'll be ok, Mom. I'll keep you posted, and try and call on Christmas Day, ok?"

"If you're sure. Are you sure?"

"Yes, I'm sure. And now, I need to go because I have a lot to do."

We hung up, and I took my plate to the sink. I washed my dishes, and went upstairs to check my email and get ready to leave.

The lavender down comforter on my bed, combined with my hangover and the greasy breakfast, called me back to take a nap.

I looked at my phone as I pulled the covers up over my head. Eleven-thirty. I would just sleep for an hour.

"Cat? Are you still sleeping?"

"Huh? What?" I sat up in bed, the towel askew on my head. Reaching for my phone, I saw it was almost four in the afternoon, and it was getting dark. Throwing the covers aside, I jumped out of bed. "Oh. My God! I must have fallen back asleep. I need to get going."

Erin was standing in my doorway, arms crossed, leaning against the door jam and looking confused. "Where are you going?"

"I'm going to Lopez Island for Christmas, and Shaye said there was a six o'clock ferry. It looks like I'm going to miss it." I stopped my running around and sat back down on the bed.

"Wow! A lot transpired since I left this morning." She laughed and pushed herself off the doorjamb, walked to me, and crawled up on my bed to sit next to me.

"Right?" I told her about my phone call with Shaye, and how I just felt like it was the right thing for me to do.

"But why? You'll be all alone."

"I don't know. It just feels like...like I need to go away. And you won't be here. I don't want to have to listen to my mom baby *me* when everyone should be enjoying my brother and the *new* baby, so I'm just gonna go. And I'll spend the week up there.

"But you'll be alone," she said again.

"I know. It's fine," I said. "It's fine!" I said again more emphatically.

"Are you sure?"

"I'm positive, Erin. I'll be fine. Shaye said she sent me an email. I'll check it in a minute, and I'll worry about things when I get up there."

She looked pensive and sad for me. "Ok. Well, do you need any help?"

"Actually, I do. Would you run down to the basement and grab my smaller suitcase? It should have a duffel bag in it."

She left my room and headed down the stairs.

While she did that task for me, I went to my computer in the other room to check my email. Shaye's was at the top of my inbox, and she had listed the ferry schedule and directions to the house.

I looked at the clock in the lower corner of my computer and confirmed that I would, most definitely, miss the six o'clock ferry. The next one was at 9:45. Hmm, that was kind of late.

I sat back in my chair to stare out the window. I thought to myself, *Maybe I should wait until the morning.*

"Is it this the one?" Erin was standing in the hall with my small suitcase. I turned at her voice, and realized I didn't want to wait until morning. I made up my mind to go.

"Yes. Thank you!" Clicking on the print button, I took the copy from the printer, and shut down the laptop. I put it in my computer bag, and went back into my room to pack.

Walking into my closet, I grabbed jeans, leggings, my winter boots, and my tennis shoes. I kept my hats and gloves in a basket on the floor, and I pulled it out from under my hanging clothes, took a beanie cap and some mittens out of it, and pushed it back under the clothes with my foot.

Out of my dresser, I grabbed some long underwear and long-sleeved t-shirts. I threw them on the bed, counting them out to make sure I had enough for many days.

I didn't think to ask if she had a washing machine, but it was a fully functioning house that they rented out, so I had to assume that she did.

The trunk of my Fiat Spider was very small, so I'm not always able to take very much with me on trips, sometimes having to load up the passenger seat.

Grabbing all my toiletries, I shoved them into a bag as well.

Erin had sat down in the oversized stuffed chair in my room to watch me pack, and I told her I would miss her.

Making small talk while I packed, I asked her how her lunch went with Perry.

She had her feet tucked under her. "It was good. He's a really nice guy."

A cheesy grin was crossing her face, and I chuckled at her slight blush.

Pausing, I watched her face soften.

"Wow! You certainly benefited from my crumbling world."

She laughed. "Stop it, your world is not crumbling. A new door is opening. And yes, I like him. I told him I would call him after the holidays, when I got back from seeing my parents."

I was a little scattered, ticking my "to-do" list off in my head. It was completely dark now. Today was the winter's solstice, and being this far north in the United States, we had really short days this time of year.

Erin stood from the chair, walking towards me to give me a hug. "I'll let you finish and I'll see you when you get back. Are you sure this is what you want to do?"

"I'm sure. I'm fine. I'll text you tomorrow, if I can. I don't know what kind of coverage they have up there, but I'll do my best to check in and let you know I arrived."

I finished packing my small suitcase with sweaters and shirts, and zipped up the bag.

She squeezed me again, hard. "You really were so funny last night."

"Right? At least maybe something good will come from my drunk-dialing."

She laughed at me on her way out of my room, and left me to finish packing.

I'd never been to the San Juan Islands before. Most of my time as a child had been spent skiing in the winter, and visiting Lake Chelan in the summer. This was a place I'd never visited, and I was kind of excited.

Placing my duffel bag and suitcase in the trunk, and my computer bag and purse on the passenger seat, I drove away from my house to spend Christmas alone.

Heading down the hill to Westlake Avenue, I drove around the south end of Lake Union to the interstate entrance, heading north toward the ferry.

It was Saturday, and the traffic was light, but I expected it to take me a few hours to get to the ferry dock. An hour into my drive, my stomach growled, and I exited the freeway to get something to eat and check the directions.

Parking in front of the convenience store attached to a Church's Chicken, I started to think this might have been a really bad idea. Anxious to leave my house, I hadn't really thought through the rest of the evening.

I threw a scarf over my computer in the passenger seat, stepped out of my car, locked it, and went into the fluorescent-lit building.

Hot dogs spun on rotating bars, and a warming tray held what looked to be burritos, but they were dry and shriveled, so I wasn't sure.

"Good evening," the clerk greeted me, and he seemed friendly.

Crossing my arms in front of me, I smiled back at him, and continued over to the walk-in coolers to grab a bottle of water.

I perused the snack aisles for something I could eat. This was such a bad idea. Maybe I was too hasty in my decision.

There was nothing good for me to eat, and I felt tears pricking my eyes. My hangover, the late hour, and the horrible lighting all made me feel worn out and alone.

Finally settling on some beef jerky and a bag of cashews, I took my purchases to the counter and paid cash. I re-entered my car with my snacks, and pep-talked myself into driving the rest of the way to the ferry dock.

Arriving at the dock a few hours later, it was almost deserted. The wind had picked up, and the trees were throwing their shadows around the parking lot.

There were only a handful of cars in line, and I decided I would stay in my car until the ferry arrived. It was quiet, and no one was out.

When the ferry arrived, only a few cars disembarked. They started loading our cars, and I ended up in front as they haphazardly loaded the vehicles across the bow of the boat.

Pulling away from the dock, the ferry chugged across the dark, deep waters of Puget Sound. I could barely make out the shapes of the islands as we passed through the channels.

The water was choppy, and the boat swayed from side to side from the force of the wind. Water crashed over the bow.

I stayed in my car for the forty-five minute boat ride, and as we approached the dock a little sideways, I sat up straighter in my car, wondering what on earth was happening. The boat appeared to be about ready to crash straight into the pilings.

"Holy crap!" I said out loud. "Does he know what he's doing?" I looked to my left and my right, at the drivers of the other cars, and they looked like they were sleeping. Was this kind of docking common?

The ferry worker, in a brown jacket with yellow reflectors, was already standing at the bow, relaxing his foot against a rope cleat, ready to unhook the orange mesh. I knew he couldn't hear me, but it made me feel better to express my concern. He didn't appear to be as worried as I was, but I kept my wide eyes on the dock, until—at the last minute— the captain turned the boat straight and gently cradled the ferry in between the pilings. What a strange experience: so tense, and then...nothing.

Churning up the water, the boat stayed in place, and the dock worker lowered the apron to the bow of the ferry. The ferry worker waved his arm at me, and I drove off   up the boat ramp and onto the road.

Up a hill, and then straight through the center of the island, I drove in complete darkness, the trees and road illuminated only by the headlights on my car. There weren't any street lights or stop lights, and I drove until I saw a gravel road where I could pull off and check the directions again.

It seemed like I was going in the right direction, but everything was so dark that I was a little disoriented.

Following the main road for another few miles, I finally came across the street I needed to turn onto. The hill was steep, and the road wound up through the cedar and pine trees lining it.

Ahead of me, I saw the stone gate that Shaye said would most likely be locked. She had given me a code, and, rolling down my window, I punched it into the metal box. The wrought-iron gate slid open, clanging against the rollers as it moved.

The road turned to gravel, and I drove at a slow pace until I saw a split in the road. Stopping, I turned on the overhead light and checked her instructions again. The house was going to be the third driveway on the left. Turning off the light, I waited a moment until my eyes adjusted to the darkness, and then slowly drove until I saw the driveway. I put my foot on the gas, as instructed, to make it up the steep driveway.

At the top of the hill was an incredibly huge house. *Why did she call it a cabin?* This house stood three stories tall with floor-to-ceiling windows. "Dang!"

Parking in front of the back steps, I turned off the ignition, and was immediately submerged in darkness. The house was dark, the trees created a canopy over the roof, and there weren't any stars out because of the cloud cover. I felt a moment of panic and fear. Oh my God, I was going to be out here all alone!

I sat for a moment in my car, and then located the flashlight app on my phone. Stepping out of the car, I walked up the steps, flashing the light around the porch until I located the old coke bottle container where Shaye had said a key would be hiding.

A butterfly key chain holder shined at me, and I stood to insert it in to the lock. The door opened, and a stained-glass picture rattled on the glass window.

Taking a few steps into the hall, I flashed the light on the wall, looking for a porch light switch.

I had just located the switch, when a shape came around the corner and tackled me to the ground. Hitting the floor with a thud, I let out a blood-curdling scream as a heavy weight landed on top of me, knocking the wind right out of me.

5

The stranger in the night had me pinned down with my hands held over my head. The weight of what I assumed to be a man straddling me, was pressing down on me, and I started kicking with my knees at his back. I opened my mouth to scream again, and the fear had paralyzed me. All that came out was a squeak.

He was immovable, and had lowered himself on my thighs so that I could no longer kick him. Fear was replaced with pleading, and I started to whimper, "Please don't hurt me. Please."

My phone had fallen to the floor near the door, and the flashlight was pointing straight at the ceiling, casting his face in shadow above me.

"Who are you? What are you doing in this house?" Oddly, I felt a moment of attraction to his voice, and I became aware of his thighs pressed up against me, heat absorbing into my middle.

"My friend Shaye said I could stay here for the holidays. She said they use it as a vacation rental, but that it was going to be empty." I felt his hands relaxing against my wrists, and he released me, rolling off me to the side.

I took that moment to scramble away from him, kicking him again, reaching for my phone, and trying to get to the back door in a half-crawling run. He grabbed me by the ankles to stop my kicking, and I tripped, rolling to my knees again, and crumbling back to the ground.

"I'm sorry. I'm not going to hurt you. I think there's been a mistake." He let go of my ankle, and I turned over to sit on my bottom, my back flush against the door.

I saw him rise, and I pulled my knees into my chest, cowering, still not even sure who he was. He flipped the light switch, an overhead light illuminating the hallway, and oh my God! This guy was gorgeous! He stood above me, bare feet, gray sweatpants hung low on his hips, and a T-shirt with a faded Indian motorcycle logo.

I sat frozen, my eyes wide. "Who the hell are you?"

"Kirin. Kirin Anderson. And you are?"

I said the first thing that popped to mind. "Meredith Gray." I don't know where that came from. I just knew I was still scared, and I didn't know who this guy was.

Hands on hips, he laughed at me—and his smile! Christ! It was disarming.

Reaching out to help me up, he said, "Okay, Meredith. We'll go with that. Come on, I won't hurt you." He put his hand to his heart. "I promise."

Tentatively, I gave him my hand, and he hauled me to my feet, coming up close to him in the small hallway.

"Ok?"

I eyed him warily.

"Let's get you something to drink." I watched his backside walk into the kitchen to my left, trying with great difficulty to avoid looking at the tight glutes moving beneath the sweatpants.

I looked down at the ground and, finally acknowledging my surroundings, noticed that the hallway led into what appeared to be the living room. I wandered into the room, and turning in a circle, I stared up at incredibly high ceilings and three stories of floor-to-ceiling windows that looked out into the forest. A catwalk crossed the vaulted space over-head, and I saw a door upstairs that I assumed to be the master bedroom, and on the other side, another hall that would lead to more rooms.

A Christmas tree that was decorated in children's ornaments and decorative plastic candy canes had been set up in the corner.

He called loudly from the kitchen, "Sit there for a bit. It'll take a few minutes for the adrenaline to leave your body."

In a bit of a daze, I said quietly to myself, "Uh-huh."

I walked around another corner through a dining room that connected to the kitchen and saw him leaning against the counter waiting for a kettle to boil. His arms were crossed over his chest, accentuating his biceps. He looked tan—unusually tan for this time of year.

"I don't understand. I just talked to Shaye this morning, and she said there wouldn't be anyone here. I really needed to get away for Christmas and be alone."

"I gathered that, and yes, I think there's been a misunderstanding."

The pot whistled, and he removed it from the stove, pouring water into a large mug with a tea bag in it. He was dipping it up and down in the mug.

"Who are you?"

"I'm a friend of Nick's." He moved his head side-to-side. "Well, kind of a friend of Nick's. A friend of mine is the sister of one of his employees."

I raised my eyebrows at him.

"That sounds dubious, doesn't it?"

"A little."

"I needed to get away as well, and I was told that I could come here. So, yeah, looks like we have a bit of a problem."

I pulled out my phone. "I'm going to call Shaye." The time on my phone read 11:49, and I hesitated. I had no idea what time her plane landed, I was kind of tired, and I figured she'd be exhausted from traveling all day with the kids, too.

He saved me from making a decision when he said, "Let's call them tomorrow."

Carrying the tea into the dining room, he placed it on the heavy oak table, and pulled a chair out for me. "Sit. You need to unwind. I'm sorry I scared you."

I eyed him warily while he waited patiently for me to cross the room. His hair was jet black, and it sprung up on his head in gentle curls that I wanted to stick my fingers in just to feel the softness. He had what looked to be a weeks' worth of a beard, and green eyes stared back at me.

He tilted his head and looked at me kindly, gesturing for me to sit down.

Warily, I sat in the chair he had pulled out for me, and he took a seat to my right, crossing his arms on the table, and stifling a yawn.

Continuing to dunk my tea bag in the water a few more times, I pulled it out and squeezed it, and he handed me a napkin to place it on.

"So, who's your friend? A girlfriend?" He raised his brows at me, and I blushed. "I'm sorry, I didn't mean to pry."

"It's ok. And no, not a girlfriend, just a friend. Her brother works for Nick."

I nodded at him, and rolled my lips between my teeth so that I wouldn't say anything else ridiculous.

He waited while I took a tentative sip of the hot tea, and then said. "You'll need to find someplace to go in the morning."

I put my mug down hard on the table, the contents splashing up to hit my hand. "I will not be going anyplace else. I don't have anywhere to go!"

"Ok, ok. Tell you what, I was sleeping when I heard you drive up. Why don't we get you settled for the night, and we can figure this out in the morning? Do you have anything you want to bring in?"

I felt tears in my eyes, and the lump in my throat prevented me from being able to speak, so I just nodded.

I felt his eyes on me for a moment, and then he rose from the table. Crossing through the kitchen, he went into the hall and came back a minute later wearing a dark gray down jacket. He slipped his feet into fur-lined boots.

Flipping on the porch light, he opened the back door. "You coming?"

I dragged myself exhaustedly from the chair, and followed wordlessly behind him, down the back steps to my car.

"How do you fit anything in this thing?"

"I didn't think I would need very much." I popped the trunk, and he grabbed both my bags. Opening the passenger door, I grabbed my computer bag from the seat, and then gently shut the door, locking it with the click of my key.

We went silently into the house, and I was aware of his presence behind me. It felt like he was everywhere. Oddly, I was more afraid of these feelings I had than I was of him. He was incredibly sexy, and his moves were fluid, like he didn't have time to waste on unnecessary activity.

He followed me into the house, and shut the door behind me, flipping off the porch light and locking the door. I didn't realize I'd gasped until he chuckled.

"Mer…" he started to say, and then stopped. With mild impatience, he asked, "What is your name?"

"Caitlyn. Caitlyn Darling."

"I'm flattered at the endearment, but shouldn't we wait to get to know each other a little better?"

"It's my last name. And I go by Cat."

Mischievously, he said, "Well, Cat. Darling. Let me show you to the back room."

Moving past me, he went towards the living room and turned right towards two back bedrooms.

We stepped into a tiny room. A queen bed took up most of the space, but there was also a nightstand and a dresser.

Placing my suitcases in the middle of the floor, he turned and almost knocked me over.

I had to grab him for balance, and he held on to my elbows. Looking up into his green eyes, I saw a flash of desire, and he pulled me a bit closer, my chest brushing up against him.

Just as quickly as I saw it, it was gone, and he stepped back, releasing me. "Sorry about that. I didn't realize you were right behind me."

I stared at him blankly.

"I think this should work for you tonight. I've been staying upstairs, so I'm not really sure what all's in here." He was looking around, taking in the scant furnishings. "The bathroom's right around the corner, and it's a full bath."

Was he rambling?

"If you need anything, I'll be upstairs."

I stood in the middle of the tiny room, and he had to scoot past me to leave. I flinched, and he must have interpreted my reaction as fear because he said gently, "I won't hurt you, Cat. I promise. I'm sorry about this mix up, and we'll fix it tomorrow. Lock the door if you need to. I understand. I'll turn the hall light on, and I'll see you in the morning."

"Thank you for the help."

He stood in the door frame. "You're welcome."

"And thanks for not killing me."

He laughed, "Sorry I startled you."

"Good night."

"You can call me Kirin."

"Good night, Kirin."

"Good night, Cat."

He turned and left my room, and I heard his feet padding up the stairs. The catwalk creaked with his weight as he crossed it to the master bedroom. I heard the door click shut, but I didn't hear a lock. Obviously, he wasn't afraid of me.

I started unpacking my suitcase, and then stopped. I wasn't even sure what I was doing tomorrow.

I took my toiletries into the bathroom, switched on the light, and gasped! My skin looked splotchy and dry, and I definitely needed a good night sleep. No way did I see desire on his face for this hot mess.

I went through my evening routine, and then I turned off the light and went back into the bedroom. I did lock the door behind me, and then I pulled back the covers on the bed.

Ohhhh, these are nice sheets, I thought to myself. Snuggling into the luxurious bedclothes, I reached out to turn off the lamp on the nightstand, and buried myself under the covers. I was out.

"Where am I?" I woke a little dazed and confused. I'd slept so hard that I felt uncertain of where I was. I rolled to my back, blinked my eyes open, and looked around at the room I was sleeping in. It was a cozy, rustic room, small but comfy. Memories of last night—and my arrival—pushed their way to the front of my mind, and I let out a small groan, turning my head to stare out the window in the corner to the forest beyond. It was so quiet. I could almost hear the pine needles dropping to the forest floor.

Smells of wood smoke, coffee, and bacon reached my nose, and my mouth began to water. The rest of the cabin was quiet. Tension grabbed me, and I lay frozen in the bed. I knew I had to get up, but I wasn't sure if I wanted to see him.

He was an unexpected surprise, and I didn't know what to make of him. I threw my forearm over my eyes. What a mess!

I rolled to my side and grabbed my phone off the nightstand. Twelve fifteen!? Good Lord! At least my hangover was gone, and my head felt a little clearer. Now, I just needed a cup of coffee.

Rolling out of bed, I placed my feet on very plush green carpet. *I missed a lot last night*, I thought to myself. I took a pair of gray leggings, and thick wool socks out of my suitcase and put them on. Padding to the bathroom, I washed my face and pulled my hair back into a low ponytail.

Walking tentatively out into the main house, I saw Kirin sitting in a brown recliner in the corner of the living room next to the Christmas tree.

A fire was lit in the blue ceramic wood-burning stove, a chimney pipe running all the way to the top of the high ceiling, and out of the room.

Kirin was reading a book, and had on a pair of reading glasses. I stopped, leaned against the wall, crossed my arms in front of me, and stared at him unabashedly. He was even prettier in the daylight. I waited until he noticed me in the hallway.

When he took off his glasses and put his book down, I gave a little wave.

"Good morning." Kirin was smiling at me.

I started to speak, but the words were stuck in my throat. I cleared it, and responded. "Hey."

"Did you sleep okay?"

"Yes, thank you."

"I made coffee and bacon, although you may need to heat it up. And there are bagels on the counter—if you eat bread."

That made me smile. This was oddly surreal, and comforting, and confusing. "Thank you."

I knew one of us had to go, but it felt comfortable, and he seemed peaceful and apparently very nice.

Turning, I went down the hall I'd come in through last night, and let out a little giggle. In the daylight, the house was not quite as ominous as it had appeared just over twelve hours ago.

In the kitchen, I noticed he had put a mug out in front of the coffee pot for me. Cream, sugar, and equal were set out, and I tore open a yellow packet and added it to the mug with a splash of cream, pouring the coffee over it. Stirring it with the spoon on the tray next to the pot, I set the spoon back down, and with two hands wrapped around the mug, walked back into the living room.

I stared at him across the room, and he stared back. He hadn't picked his book back up, and he appeared to be waiting for me.

He gestured to another recliner directly across from him, this one facing out to the woods and backing up against a handmade wooden console.

"Why don't you sit and enjoy the..." He paused and looked at his fancy black watch. Smiling at me, he finished his sentence. "Well, the afternoon."

His voice was soothing, and he was ridiculously attractive. I felt his words resonate in my chest, and defensively, I said, "You know you can't stay here."

He laughed and nodded. "Yes, and we can talk about that when you're fully awake."

Cautiously, I went to the chair, put my mug down on the end table, sat down, and pulled a cream-colored Irish-knit

blanket over my legs. I put my hand to
the side to pull the lever that would lift
the foot-rest and adjusted the blanket
over my feet. Reaching over for my mug,
and holding it with two hands, I drank
the hot liquid, and felt it seep into my
cells.

I closed my eyes, and hummed.
"This is so good."

His back was to the window, so he
couldn't see the view, but it was
stunning. The weight of the dew was
drooping the branches of the pine and fir
trees. The fog was low in the trees and
created a blanket around the cabin.

He had gone back to reading his
book, and I glanced surreptitiously at
him.

Curiosity got the best of me and I
interrupted him. "What do you do?"

Lowering his book, he removed his
glasses...*again*, and gave me a half-smile.
"I'm a screenwriter."

"Why are you here?"

"I wanted some peace and quiet.
Why are you here?"

"Peace and quiet." Our words sat
between us for a minute. He continued to

watch me, waiting for me to elaborate, so I asked "Did you talk to Nick yet?"

"No. I was waiting for you to get up to see what you wanted to do."

I fidgeted a little in the chair. I wanted to be here, but I didn't want to be here with him. On the other hand, I found his presence calming, and kind of did want to be with him, and that confused me.

"Shaye said there was a really nice place to hike around here. I've never been here before so maybe..." I paused, watching his reaction, and his smile grew, making me feel flushed. "Maybe I'll send her an email, stay another day while I wait for her response."

He grinned at me knowingly. "That sounds fair. I like that plan." Which simultaneously irked, and intrigued me. He appeared to not even be concerned that he might be the one to leave—also, that he might not want me to leave either. I watched as he picked up his book and continued to read.

"How come you don't have a car here?"

This time he closed his book, a look of affectionate tolerance on his face, and put it on the floor next to him.

"I had someone drop me off. I didn't think I would have a need to go anywhere, and they will come and get me when I'm ready."

I laughed at him. "That's awfully elitist of you."

A flash of wariness crossed his face, but he remained silent, which made me curious.

"Ok, then," I said almost to myself. I threw the blanket off me and put the recliner back into its original position. Standing, I took my coffee mug to the kitchen, and then headed back towards the back bedroom.

"Are you going somewhere?" he called after me.

Poking my head back around the corner, I said, "I thought I might try and find that place Shaye mentioned. I think it would be a good place to go for a walk, and then I might head into town to look around."

He leaned forward, putting his recliner back into a sitting position. "I'll go with you."

"I didn't invite you."

"But you have a car, and I need something." And with that, he went past me and headed up the stairs to his room, leaving me staring at his backside. Again.

Shaking my head, I drawled to no one, "Okay."

The bathroom was cold, so I turned the space heater on while I showered. I really needed to send an email to Shaye. I wanted to be alone. I needed to be alone.

Wrapped in a towel, I went to my room, sat on the bed, and opened my laptop. I sent a quick email to Shaye, letting her know about my squatter, and hoped she responded today. Email sent, I shut the laptop and rifled through my suitcase, looking for something to wear. I settled on black leggings and a gray wool tunic-sweater.

In the bathroom, I blow-dried my hair and applied some makeup. This was ridiculous! This was not a date. Huffing to myself, I finger fluffed my hair, and left the bathroom.

I grabbed my purple knit cap and my wool coat, and went to the dining room to wait for him.

Shaye's instruction email was sitting on the table where I'd left it last night. The hiking area looked to be just a mile or so from the house, an easy walk to a small beach. I heard the catwalk creaking with the weight of Kirin's steps, and then his feet came thumping quickly down the stairs.

He stepped into the kitchen, and my eyes widened, and my stomach dropped. He had trimmed his beard, and his hair was still wet from his shower. He was wearing belted, low-rise jeans, and hikers on his feet. I licked my lips, imagining the sexy V he hopefully had on his abs. Raising my eyes, I noticed a navy knit turtleneck, the sleeves pushed up to his elbows. When my eyes finally made it to his face, he was smiling at me, his eyes crinkling at the corners.

Quickly dropping my eyes to the paper, I said, "The hiking area is just a short way from here, so maybe we can go there first."

He sat next to me and leaned against my shoulder so that he could read the directions. His shoulder pressed up against mine, and I held my breath.

Turning to look at me, his eyes dropped to my mouth. "Sure, we can do that."

I pushed back in my chair and stood abruptly. "I sent an email to Shaye."

"Good, hopefully we'll have this all cleared up by tonight." His grin was too big and too charming.

"Don't patronize me. This isn't funny. I wanted to be alone, and now you're here, looking all—well, looking all..." I waved my finger frantically, pointing it all around, my hand waving up and down him. "Looking all like you do, and I don't appreciate it."

"You don't appreciate how I look?" He looked down at his outfit.

I huffed, and grabbed my purse off the back of the chair, ignoring his question. "Let's go."

He followed me out the door and down the steps to my car. Before stepping into the passenger side, he looked over the roof of my car and said, "I'm sorry about the mix-up Cat. I really am. But this is a really beautiful place, and you should take a few minutes to enjoy it."

I had opened my driver side door and paused to listen to him. When I didn't immediately respond, he continued. "I know you wanted to be alone, but in the meantime, let's just have a nice afternoon, okay?"

He had a point. It wasn't his fault, and he had been nothing but kind to me. Well, except for scaring the shit out of me when he tackled me. I nodded at him. "Get in." I was rewarded with a grin that spread across his face.

The map led us to a secluded parking lot with a sign indicating it was a half mile to the beach.

We sat in the car, the heater blasting warm air on us. He turned in the car to face me, and I caught a hint of warm, woodsy body wash. "Ready to go?"

I stared out to the front window to the path ahead. "It looks really cold out there."

He waited for me to continue, his forearm on the arm rest.

I bit my lower lip. "Maybe we just go into town?"

"Whatever you want to do. I'm along for the ride, and chocolate."

"Chocolate?"

"Yes. I have a craving for something sweet."

"You're ridiculous!"

He leaned closer and grinned widely. "Yeah, but you like me!"

I could see his incisors almost had a fang look to them. "We're stuck together for now, but don't get any ideas."

He chuckled, and sat back in his seat. I put the car in reverse to back out of the parking area, and he said boldly, "To the store!"

In the daylight, it was much easier to navigate the island roads. The fir and pine tree forests of the south end of the island opened to fields of sheep.

We drove through a quiet village, quaint and almost deserted of visitors. A strip center of six small shops, ranging from a pizza place to a real estate office, appeared to be closed today. At the end of the street was the law office that belonged to Shaye's husband. We circled around past a post office, a liquor store, and a bank, and pulled into the grocery store parking lot. Only a few cars were there, and I wondered about the population of the island. It seemed so deserted.

Turning off the car, I stepped out and waited for Kirin to open the passenger door and unfold himself before I remote-locked it. It beeped, and I noticed a gentleman at the gas pump give me a strange look.

Kirin walked beside me as we entered the store, and I grabbed a grocery cart. Holiday decorations were displayed at the front of the store, and Kirin picked up a plastic sprig of mistletoe. "Do we need this?"

"No, you're leaving tomorrow. Didn't you want some chocolate or something?" I turned from him and went to the fruit and vegetable section.

I heard him laugh behind me, and he wandered off in the opposite direction.

The golden delicious apples looked crisp and sweet, and I grabbed two of them. Unsure if I would need dinner or not, I picked out some tomatoes and lettuce, making a mental note to grab some garden burgers from the organic frozen food section.

Kirin appeared back at my side with a box of clementine oranges, and he put them in the cart. He had a small grocery bag in his other hand.

"Did you find some chocolate?"

"I did. I found Toblerone. It's more than chocolate."

"Are you going to share?"

He leaned in close to me and whispered, "If you're nice."

I stopped the cart, and turned so that I could look at him straight. He had been flirting with me all morning, so I finally flirted right back. Slowly scanning him from his toes to the top of his head, I finally said, "Huh. Maybe."

I walked off, and he laughed behind me. "Oh my God! I feel violated."

He followed behind me, and I bossily said over my shoulder, "Go get me some hamburger buns."

"Are you cooking me dinner?" he called after me.

"Yes, and then you're leaving tomorrow."

He met me at the checkout counter. The cashier looked like she was probably still in high school.

Kirin greeted her cheerily, "Merry Christmas!"

This guy's smile could melt the polar ice caps. "Merry Christmas." She flushed dark red. I felt her pain.

"It's awfully quiet here," I said to ease her discomfort.

"It'll get busy over New Year's Eve. We don't get many tourists over Christmas."

She continued to check out our groceries, and then Kirin pulled out his credit card to pay.

I put my hand on his forearm to stop him. "I can get it."

He looked down at my hand on his arm, and then raised his eyes to me. "I can get it, Cat. Let me pay."

My hand stayed on his arm a fraction too long, and he simply waited.

"Thank you."

We took the groceries to the car in silence. I was feeling confused about what was happening between us.

He put the groceries in the trunk, closed it, and asked, "Do you want to get a coffee?"

I told him I thought that sounded like a good idea, and we drove the short distance to the quirky coffee shop on the corner.

We took our coffees back to the car, and I had to point out the tiny cup holder between the seats. We both turned our heads to look, and I heard him inhale. "Your hair smells really good."

I felt a rush through my body. His words were barely a whisper and I took a deep breath before rushing my next words. "I heard it's supposed to snow in Seattle this week."

He nodded, laughing a little at my change of topic. "I didn't know that. I haven't been paying attention to the news. Maybe it'll snow here, too."

We drove back in silence, the radio tuned to a Christmas station.

Kirin helped me unload the groceries, and I went to the bedroom to check my email. No message from Shaye.

Wandering back into the kitchen, I saw that he was finishing up with the dishes from this morning.

Over his shoulder he said, "Any word?"

I leaned against the door frame, watching him. "No, nothing yet."

Finishing up, he turned off the water and dried his hands. "I'm going upstairs to write for a bit. Let me know if you hear anything, ok?"

His eyes were void of emotion, and I felt as if there was something I should say. We continued looking at each other, and I shifted my weight off the door frame to stand straight.

"Kirin?"

"I'll come back down in a couple of hours and help you with dinner."

"Okay. Thank you for keeping me company today."

He put his lips together and nodded at me. I was blocking the way to the hall, so he went around through the living room to the stairs. I felt a sense of loss that he wasn't staying downstairs with me.

I went into the living room and laid down on the couch. The sky was darkening, and it was only a little after three in the afternoon. I rested my head on a pillow, stared out at the forest beyond the tall glass windows, and allowed my eyes to slowly close.

Soft music was playing in my dream, and I felt Sam pressed up against me. I rolled to my side, pressed my hips into his, and rested my hands on his legs, trying to curl around him.

"Sam."

A gentle hand brushed my hair back from my face, and then settled on my shoulder. "Cat, wake up."

Slowly, I opened my eyes, focusing dazedly on the face that was definitely not Sam's. "Kirin?"

"Who's Sam?"

His voice was gentle, and tears welled in my eyes before I could respond. I rolled over onto my back, pulling a blanket up to my chin.

"I'm guessing he's the reason you're here?"

I nodded, the knot in my throat making it difficult to speak.

"Do you want me to bring you a glass of wine?"

"Yes..." I cleared my throat, and sat up. "Yes, please."

"I'll be right back."

He went into the kitchen, and I looked around the room. The Christmas tree had been plugged in, and the lights were twinkling off the glass of the windows, reflecting back at me. It was dark outside, and Kirin had lit a fire and turned on the lamps, giving the room a cozy, romantic feel.

Kirin returned with my wine, and I noticed he was barefoot. His jeans were rolled up at the hem, and his gray hoodie sweatshirt made him look snuggly.

"Here you go." He placed the glass on the end table and sat back down on the edge of the couch.

Reaching for the glass, I thanked him and took a relaxing sip.

"You hungry?"

"A little."

"I didn't want you to sleep too long, or you wouldn't sleep tonight."

"That was nice of you."

His eyes were searching mine, waiting, I'm sure, for an explanation about Sam.

When I didn't say any more, he continued. "Why don't I cook us up the garden burgers, and you can sit here for a minute and wake up?"

"Ok."

He went back into the kitchen, and, instead of resting, I took my wine and went into the back bedroom to check my emails.

Shaye had responded, and there had, indeed, been a mix-up. She was incredibly apologetic. I shut the cover of my laptop and went into the kitchen to help Kirin.

"Do you need any help?"

He turned at the sound of my voice and grinned at me, his face lighting up. "Sure! Why don't you slice the tomatoes and lettuce? I'll toast the buns just before the burgers are ready." His brow creased, and he asked, "Do you like toasted buns?"

Laughing at his juvenile innuendo, I crossed the room to the refrigerator to get the lettuce and tomatoes, and responded sexily. "I like toasted buns."

We worked silently together, the music playing in the background, and at one point, I heard him move behind me. He reached around me and poured more wine in my glass, and I almost leaned back into him. Instead, I tilted my chin and looked up at him. "Thank you."

He glanced at my mouth, smiled, and simply nodded.

I pulled out a container of potato salad from the refrigerator and placed it on the table with the vegetables, while Kirin finished with the garden burgers and the toasted buns. A pine-scented candle was in the center of the table, and I lit it with an electric lighter that was placed next to it. I brought our wine glasses to the table, sat down, and waited for him to join me.

"Your dinner is served, Cat, darling." With flair, he placed a plate in front of me.

"This looks great! Thank you for cooking."

"No problem."

I put lettuce and tomatoes on my burger, while he served up the potato salad.

We ate in silence, and I waited until he had taken a few bites before I told him about Shaye's email.

"Shaye responded."

He finished chewing and asked, "What did she say?"

"She said she thought her husband said that you were staying in their house while they were away. She misunderstood him. So, when I talked to her, she thought the cabin was empty."

He was waiting for me to continue, and he took another bite of his burger.

With a full mouth, he said, "I'm not usually a fan of garden burgers, but these are pretty good."

I continued, even though he didn't seem to be too interested in the outcome. "She offered their house to me and gave me directions." I paused when I knew he was listening. "I'll leave in the morning."

He nodded quietly. When he looked at me, I saw affection, and something else. I was so confused. I didn't really want to leave, but now that I realized the mistake, I couldn't very well impose on his holiday.

He wiped his mouth with a napkin, and took a sip of his wine. "Now you'll have your peace and quiet."

"I guess so."

He cleared his throat and said, "Maybe if you've had enough 'quiet space'…" he made air quotes and continued, "…we can spend Christmas together. I mean, since we'll both still be on the island, and we're alone."

"Sure, maybe." I picked up my burger, and took another bite, trying to force down the tears I felt welling up.

"It is kind of sad that we were planning on spending Christmas alone in the first place." His eyes never left my face, and his gentle tone caused my tears to fall.

"Why are you crying, Cat?" He pushed his plate away, and leaned forward on the table.

I shook my head to try and compose myself, taking a sip of my wine and letting out a breath I didn't realize I'd been holding.

"It's a long story."

He nodded, waited a few minutes, and then stood to take his plate to the sink. "Are you finished?"

Handing him my plate, I thanked him and blew out the candle.

"Why don't you go sit by the fire? I'll clean up in here and bring you a brandy."

"Brandy? Where have you been hiding that?" I stood and smiled at him.

"I came prepared."

"For damsels in distress?"

He simply shrugged and went to the sink to wash our dinner dishes.

Now that I was fully awake and fed, I could appreciate the beauty of the living room. The Christmas tree lights and the soft lamp lighting relaxed me, and I briefly thought I might have made a mistake in not spending the holidays with my family.

I sat down at the end of the couch where I'd been sleeping, curled my legs up under me, and stared into the fire. It wasn't difficult to imagine why Shaye had moved here. It was beautiful. Well, that, and maybe her husband had something to do with it.

Lost in my musings, I didn't notice that Kirin had come back into the living room until he was directly in front of me, a brandy snifter in his hand.

Reaching up to take it from him, I thanked him, and he sat down at the other end of the couch.

A blanket sat between us, and I reached out to pull it over my legs. I could feel his eyes on me, and he was making me nervous. The fire and the brandy were warming me, and I was starting to imagine kissing him.

I turned my head to him and saw a sly smile on his face, his head resting in his hand, his elbow on the back of the couch.

"What?"

"Nothing."

"Why are you looking at me like that?"

He laughed, lifted his head, and took a small sip of his brandy. "Like what?"

"Like you find this situation funny."

"It is funny." His grin turned cheesy, and I turned back to the fire. "And you look really pretty right now."

My heart rate sped up, and I couldn't look at him. I felt my face flush, and was grateful for the dim lighting so that he wouldn't see how his words were affecting me.

A moment passed, and he said softly, "Who's Sam?"

I put my head back on the cushion and looked up towards the tall glass windows, out into the darkness of the forest beyond. Thinking through how much I would tell him, I finally rolled my head to the side so that I could see him, and started talking.

"Sam was my boyfriend."

"And he's no longer your boyfriend?"

"No." The admission made my eyes water, and I felt the tears start to fall.

He reached for a box of tissues that were on the coffee table, and handed them to me. I pulled back reflexively, startled by his closeness, and held my breath. He put the box on my lap, and scooted back to his spot on the couch.

"Thank you." I pulled a tissue from the box, and blew my nose. "Sorry about that."

"You seemed a little upset earlier."

"I'm not sure how I feel."

"How long were you together?"

"Two years."

"That's a long time."

"Yeah, I guess it is." I took a sip of my drink, and thought back on my time with him. Kirin was staring at me pensively, waiting. "We were supposed to go skiing in Aspen with his family, and when I got home from work on Friday, he'd sent me an email saying that he'd already left, and that he was breaking up with me."

Kirin's peaceful demeanor changed to one of mild anger and disbelief. "Are you kidding me?"

His vehemence made me laugh a little. "No, I'm not kidding you."

"That's a dick move if I ever heard of one."

"Yes. I agree. I had a few other choice words for him, but yeah, dick move for sure."

"Wow! I'm so sorry."

I waited for him to stop shaking his head before I continued.

"On top of that, I got fired Friday as well."

His glass was halfway to his mouth, and he paused, lowering it again, and then started laughing.

"Oh my God! Cat!"

"On top of all of that, I came here, and you're already here, so it's kind of a trifecta of bad outcomes."

His voice was silky when he said, "Ah, come on, you like me."

"You tried to kill me!"

He leaned forward, and put his hand to his heart. "I am so, *so* very sorry for scaring you. Please forgive me."

"I forgive you." We smiled at each other. I was the first to look away.

"So, what do you do? What *did* you do?"

"I'm a graphic designer."

Interest sparked in his eyes. "Really? What do you design?"

"Ad campaigns for sporting goods stores and brands."

"That's very cool! Do you like doing outdoorsy things?" He sounded like he was teasing me.

I giggled, the brandy now seeping into my body, relaxing me even more. I said, "Not at all!" and he laughed at me.

"If you don't like the outdoors, how did you end up branding for companies that specialize in that?"

"I won a contest, and it just opened the right doors. I have all the gear; I just don't use it. And I'm *very* talented." I drawled out the "very," and he raised his eyebrows at me.

"Who are some of your clients?"

"Were."

"Sorry, who were some of your clients?"

I looked down at the couch cushions, thinking through all the accounts I had brought on over the years. "Let's see: K2 skis, Outdoor Emporium, Tri-State Outfitters. Do you even know who these businesses are?"

He shook his head and gave me a broad smile. "No."

"You're ridiculous." I rested my head again, and looked at him with heavy eyes.

"What was your biggest account?"

"Patagonia." The thought of that loss brought tears to my eyes. "And now...now I have nothing."

"Hey, hey, stop that." He had scooted closer to me on the couch and put his hand on my head, smoothing my hair back. "Sometimes, the best things happen when all doors close."

"You sound like you're speaking from experience." His hand felt so lovely on my head, and he ran his fingers through my hair as he pulled it back.

"No, I just read it on a cereal box."

"You did not!"

"No, I didn't. But isn't that a saying that makes people feel better?" He was mocking me, and oddly, it was comforting.

I pulled a cream-colored throw pillow to my chest. "I guess so."

We sat in silence for a while, sipping our brandy and staring into the fire, each reflective in our own thoughts. He hadn't moved back to his spot on the couch, staying close enough to touch me, but far enough to be respectful.

Curiosity got the best of me, and I finally asked him about himself.

"Not much to tell, really. My parents have been married for 40 years. I have two brothers. One's a plastic surgeon, and the other's a NASA Engineer."

"WOW! Smarties!"

He chuckled. "I guess so."

"Is your dad a doctor?"

"Heart surgeon. And my mom's an ER nurse."

"And you're the creative one." It was a statement, and he nodded.

"I'm the creative one." He had put his head back in his hand and was smiling at me. Small lines creased the outside of his eyes endearingly.

"You aren't from Seattle," I stated, not really sure if I was waiting for confirmation, or contradiction.

"How do you know?" he teased me.

"You're unusually tan for the Northwest. Especially this time of year."

"Ah, of course. The tan." He said this in a deep voice, as if it was a mystery.

"Vacation?"

"Home."

Teasingly, I said, "You're starting to piss me off."

He sighed heavily, and then smiled at me. "I live in California. Laguna Beach."

My heart sunk a little at the realization that he lived so far away, and I felt my smile drop. He lifted his head from his hands so that he could face me straight on.

"That's a long way away." My reaction to him was confusing me. It might have been the brandy, but I desperately wanted to kiss him, and my chest felt tight.

"Kind of, yeah."

Trying to keep the conversation as neutral as possible, I continued. "I guess that makes sense if you're a screenwriter."

"Yes," he responded non-committedly.

"What are you working on?"

He leaned closer, narrowed his eyes dramatically, and whispered, "A thriller."

My eyes got wide. "Are you trying to scare me?"

He laughed boldly. "No, but that was fun to watch."

"Do I need to call your mom?"

He reached in his back pocket to get his phone. "Do you want to? She can vouch for me."

His fingers hovered over the number pad, and I swatted his hand from his phone. "No. I don't want to talk to your mom."

Placing his phone on the coffee table, he took another sip of brandy.

"So, what's the story about?"

100

He settled back into the couch and said, "It's about an actor with a stalker, and there's an attempted murder—a cult, unrequited love, and a manhunt."

Something tingled at the back of my neck. Not from fear, but something familiar. "This sounds familiar. I hate to tell you this, but I think it's been done."

"I'm putting my own spin on it. But I can't tell you what it is."

I mocked him teasingly. "Well, it better be good, or you'll be eating beans and wieners for a while."

He threw back his head and laughed out loud. "I'm sure I won't starve. And you'll just have to see the movie when it comes out."

The alarm bells got louder in my head. But again, not out of fear. Something was off. Something I couldn't quite put my finger on right now. This situation was extremely unusual, and while I should be apprehensive, I knew intuitively he wouldn't hurt me.

He must have seen a moment of panic flash across my face because he scooted closer and put his hand on my forearm. "Cat, it's just a story."

Goosebumps rose on my arm, and we both looked down to where he was touching me. His touch turned gentle, and he ran his fingers down to interlock them with mine.

My breathing sped up, and I looked up to see him glance down at my mouth again. I felt heat rush down between my legs, and I licked my lips nervously. I'd never felt like this with Sam. I felt like I was going to spontaneously combust right here on the couch.

I wasn't ready for this. Slowly pulling my fingers out of his grasp, I pulled back the blanket and casually stood up. He sat back against the cushions, feet firmly planted on the floor, his palms flat on the tops of thighs. He looked like he was forcing himself to stay still. Sexual tension radiated between us.

"It's late." My words sounded so banal.

"Yes."

We watched each other warily. My chest was heaving, and I struggled to think of something to say—something that would reduce the tension.

"I should get to bed if I want to head over to Shaye's in the morning."

"Yes."

His word, so succinct, gave me time to clear my head. "Well, thank you for dinner."

This time, he didn't respond, just waited.

I turned to head to the back bedroom.

"Good-night, Kirin."

"Good-night, Cat."

It was too silent. The small room seemed as if it had been soundproofed overnight. Was Kirin even here? Last night had shaken my nerves, and I knew for certain that I needed to leave today, if only to get some space from the unexpected feelings Kirin was evoking.

I lay on my back, linking my fingers together, and placing my hands on my forehead. Staring up at the ceiling, I wondered how I could be feeling this way about someone after such a short time. My relationship with Sam now seemed so distant, and I wondered why I had invested so much emotional energy in him.

A soft knock sounded at my door, and adrenaline shot through my body.

"Cat?"

I sat straight up in bed and pulled the covers to my chest.

Tentatively, I responded, "Yes?"

Through the door, he said, "I made coffee. Are you hungry for breakfast?"

"Uhm, not yet. I'll be out in a minute."

"Okay. When you're ready."

The house was silent again. I couldn't even hear his footsteps. I felt frozen in place. Something wasn't right. Chewing on my bottom lip, I casually pulled the covers off of me, and swung my legs out of bed. My feet hit the carpeted floor, and I padded to the window. Turning the rod to open the blinds, I gasped. "What on Earth?"

Moving quickly to the bedroom door, I threw it open and ran out into the living room. "Kirin?"

"In here," he called from the dining area.

I ran around the corner, almost tripping over the shoes I'd left in the hall last night.

"Is that snow?" I stood, wide-eyed in front of him, as he casually lifted his eyes from his laptop to me.

"It appears to be."

"How come there's so much of it?"

He pulled his lips in between his teeth to stifle a laugh.

I ran through the kitchen towards the back door. Flinging it open, I ran out onto the back deck and wailed, "My car!"

It was buried in snow. The wheel wells were not even visible through the blanket of white.

The chill hit me, and I went back inside, shutting the door behind me and walking back into the kitchen.

Petulantly, I asked, "How am I supposed to get out of here?"

Instead of answering me, his lazy gaze rolled over me, and his eyes darkened with desire. He was no longer smiling, and it was then that I realized I was only wearing boy short panties and a camisole. The peaks of my large breasts pointed from the cold. Hot lust slammed through me at his wanton look, and I turned and ran back to my bedroom, slamming the door behind me and panting with need.

Christ almighty! What am I going to do? I sat down on the edge of the bed to think, placing my palms flat on the mattress next to me. This was so bad—so very, very bad. I half-expected him to follow me in here. Half of me wanted him to, too. The other half wanted to run far and fast.

Think, Cat! Think. Okay. The first thing I needed to do was get dressed, get some coffee in me, and then try and have a rational conversation with him.

I stood to dress in a long-sleeved turtleneck sweater, leggings, and heavy wool socks. Maybe if I had a lot of clothes on, I might be immune to whatever it was about him that was making me react this way. I wrapped a scarf around my neck, and then immediately removed it.

"Don't be ridiculous, Cat," I said to myself.

Opening the door, I went to the bathroom to brush my teeth, and then joined Kirin in the dining room.

He watched me thoughtfully as I pulled out a chair at the table and sat down.

His eyes were crinkled at the sides, and I felt relieved that he was, once again, laughing at me.

"So."

"So," he repeated, and his grin grew.

"I appear to be stuck here."

He pulled his lips in again to keep from laughing at me, and nodded.

"Do you think there is someone I can call who can plow the roads? Dig my car out?"

"There's a phone book on the counter over there, under the red wall phone. You might find something in there."

Pushing back from the table, I located the phone book and started leafing through it.

"Lopez Sand & Gravel!" I exclaimed. "It says they can clear roads. Should I call them?"

A brief flash of hurt crossed his face, and he went back to working on his laptop, mumbling, "Sure."

I dialed the number listed and waited for someone to answer.

After a few rings, a lady answered in a clipped tone.

"Oh, hello! I'm so glad you answered. My name is Cat Darling and I'm—"

She cut me off, and I turned to look at Kirin, who had also just looked back up at me.

108

"My last name is Darling." *This just never ends*, I thought to myself. "I'm snowed in at a friend's cabin, and I need to leave today."

She cut me off, and I listened to her rambling.

"Oh, ok. The address is..." I shuffled the papers that contained the email from Shaye around on the counter, and rattled off the address.

"Will you be able to...?" She hung up on me, and I held the phone away from my ear, staring at the mouthpiece, and then at Kirin. "She hung up on me."

"What did she say?"

Gently hanging the phone back on the wall, I slowly walked back to the table and sat down. Chin cradled in my palms, I said, "She said they are very busy working on the main roads, and they will do their best to get to me today. If they aren't able to make it, I'll have to wait until Thursday since tomorrow is Christmas Eve, and they are closed for two days."

I crossed my arms on the table and dropped my forehead onto them. A gentle hand reached out to touch my arm, and I turned my head sideways to look at him.

Sarcasm laced his tone. "I can't imagine a more endearing house guest to spend the holidays with."

He pulled his hand back, and I sat up in my chair, resigning myself to the fact that I was most likely going to be here for a few more days.

"Please don't take offense, but I was really looking forward to being alone."

He nodded knowingly.

"But, I guess, well—I guess you're alright." I gave him a half smile, and he grinned back at me.

"Maybe I can help you figure out what you should do next in your life."

"Are you going to write me a script?"

"I can do that. Let's feed you first, and then see what happens. We have lots of time." He stood from the table. "Is oatmeal okay for breakfast?"

"Brown sugar and butter?"

"Uh, maybe?" He looked in the cupboards, found the brown sugar, and raised it high. "Brown sugar it is."

Sipping the coffee he brought me, I watched him surreptitiously as he moved around the kitchen, cutting up fruit and

110

keeping watch over the oatmeal. A sprinkling of dark hair peeked out from above the top buttons of his maroon Henley, and his jeans were resting low on his hips, the cuffs rolled up at the bottom. His feet were bare. I found myself licking my lips.

To keep myself from drooling, I asked him about the rules of the house.

He chuckled, and said, "What do you mean, 'the rules?'"

"Since we'll most likely be here together for a few days, how do you want to split chores? And, how much time do you need to write? Are we allowed to talk to each other?"

He stopped and stared at me, spoon elevated in his hand. "Wow!"

"Wow, what?"

"You don't relax often, do you?"

His question made me realize that it had been a really long time since I'd taken a vacation. Even then, it was only a weekend away at the shore.

"I guess I don't," I mused.

He went back to stirring the oatmeal, and then he removed it from the stove to cool.

"Tell you what, whoever wakes first makes the coffee. If you want to make breakfast, or lunch, or dinner, go right ahead. And if not, I'll make it. We'll wash—and dry—the dishes together, and you can talk to me whenever you want."

"Are you sure I won't disturb you?"

He dished out the oatmeal from the pan, and put it in a bowl. Placing the bowl of oatmeal in front of me, he looked down into my eyes. "Disturb me? No. Distract me? Most definitely. But you'll do that whether you talk or not."

He went back into the kitchen to clean up, and I blew on my oatmeal, waiting for it to cool, and asked, "How much longer were you planning to be alone up here?"

"Contrary to what you might be imagining, I'm not a hermit. I enjoy being social, and I enjoy being around people."

"And yet, here you are."

"Yes."

"Yesterday you said you wanted peace and quiet."

He was silent for a moment. Drying his hands on a towel, he came back over to the table and sat down, peeling a clementine he had grabbed from a fruit bowl on the counter.

"No, I said I was here for peace and quiet, not that I wanted peace and quiet."

I had taken a bite of my oatmeal and mumbled, "Semantics."

He laughed at me, popped the small orange pieces in his mouth and mumbled back. "I'll tell you later. Promise."

Finishing my breakfast, I took my bowl to the sink and washed it, placing it in the dish rack on the right   .

I turned and asked him, "What do we do now?"

"First, we need to clear the snow from your car." I watched him walk to the candy jar on the counter, reach in, and pull out a handful of red and green foiled candy. He sauntered towards me, and I leaned back against the counter, putting more distance between us.

He kept coming until he was standing right in front of me, and my stomach fluttered.

"Do you want a kiss?"

Placing my hands on the sink behind me for balance, I looked at his mouth, and inhaled sharply.

"Uhm, sure?"

He popped a chocolate candy in his mouth and handed me a red foil wrapped candy.

Looking up into his eyes, I saw he was laughing at me again, and I pushed against his chest. "Ha-ha! Put your coat on and help me."

Stumbling backwards, he clutched his heart. "Ouch! That hurts my feelings."

I left him standing in the kitchen, his laughter following me down the hall.

When I got to my room, I let out a nervous giggle and changed into warmer clothes.

He met me at the back door, holding a pair of bulky snow boots and a large parka. "Put these on."

"I will not. I'll look ridiculous."

"This isn't a fashion show, Cat. We're going out into more than a foot of snow."

Huffing, I grabbed them from his hands, slid my feet into the boots, and put on the parka, zipping it up to my neck.

Reaching behind me for the hood, he pulled it up over my head and tightened the drawstring, the fur-lined hood framing my face.

Instinctively, I reached out to grab the front of his jacket, and we looked at each other, our emotions precariously perched on the edge of longing.

His hands reached in to cup my cheeks, his fingers gently caressing the side of my neck, and I closed my eyes, leaning towards him.

A moment later, I felt his lips touch mine, gently and tentatively. I sighed, leaning closer to him. I heard him inhale, and his mouth pressed more firmly against mine. I held onto him for balance, the sweet sensations running through me, squeezing my heart.

Too soon, he pulled back slowly, and my eyes opened heavily.

He softly ran his thumbs across my cheek, and then dropped his hands, reaching for my fingers on his coat. "C'mon, Darling, let's take care of your car."

Following behind him, the large boots encumbered my ability to walk gracefully down the steps. "How does anyone even walk in these things?"

"How are you from the Northwest and you can't?" He kept marching towards the storage shed under the deck. He said over his shoulder, "Stay right there, I'm going to look for some shovels."

Left alone, I felt a moment of serenity, the freshly fallen snow adding to the peace and quiet of the moment.

Kirin came lumbering back up from under the deck, two shovels in hand, and I stared dazedly at him as he stopped in front of me— his face so familiar, and yet not. I shook my head to clear it.

"Cat, are you ok?"

"I...yes. Yes, I'm ok. Just daydreaming, I guess."

He reached around me, picking me up, and holding me close. "C'mon then, slacker, you have work to do."

I giggled and wrapped my arms around his neck, legs dangling, as he fumbled through the snow, trying not to drop the shovels.

Dropping me unceremoniously next to the front tire, he handed me a shovel. "You do this side, I'll take the other side. Swipe the snow off the hood with your arm, and start digging out a trench along the side of the car."

He worked much faster than me, and ended up doing the back tire on my side.

"Since I had to work harder than you today, you get to make dinner."

I sighed and leaned on the shovel. "This is hard work."

He stalked towards me. "Oh, poor baby."

"What are you doing?" I asked him warily as he got closer, trying to stop the grin spreading on my face.

He scooped up some snow from the ground, and I put my hands in front of me, trying to ward him off, the shovel falling to the snow-covered ground.

"Oh, no. No, no, no you don't."

His grin spread. My God. With his dark hair and green eyes, he was so unbelievably gorgeous. My heart lurched, and I tried to back up. He lunged forward, laughing, and shoved the snow down the back of my neck. He was now close enough for me to grab his jacket front, and when I tripped backwards, landing on my back, I took him with me.

He cushioned my fall by putting his arms around me, and I let out an "OOF!" as his weight crushed me.

117

"Oh, dear God! You're heavy! Get off of me!"

He pushed off from me, his gloved hands on the ground on either side of my face, bracing himself above me, and I felt him slide his leg between mine.

Lust shot through me, and I saw my desire mirrored back at me in his eyes. His mouth crashed down onto mine, and I wrapped my arms around him, holding him close. The weight of him pressed down on me, and I lifted my booted legs to the back of his thighs. We were a perfect fit, and I instantly wanted all of my clothes off. Darting out my tongue, I tasted the seam of his mouth until he parted his lips, and our tongues clashed, heat and desire urging us on. He pulled back and unzipped my jacket, pulling off his gloves, and shoving his hands up under my sweater. "God bless, Cat. You're so fucking beautiful." His words—and the cold draft—broke the spell, and reminded me where we were. I shoved against his chest, pushing him over into the snow.

"Stop! Stop!" I scrambled out from underneath him and rolled to my hands and knees. Pushing myself off the ground, I stood, and plodded through the snow back to the steps and into the house.

"Cat! Wait!"

I kicked the boots off at the door and pulled the big coat off in the hallway.

Kirin came thundering in right behind me. "Cat!"

I turned in the hall and pointed my finger at him. "You do not get to take advantage of me! Just because I'm stuck here with you, and my heart is fragile, and you're all, well…" I pointed my finger up and down his length. "You look, all, like you do."

He had stopped at my yelling and put his hands in the air. When I lost a little bit of steam, he calmed, and a grin spread on his face.

"UGH!" I stomped off into the living room and sat down on the couch, pulling my legs up underneath me and a pillow to my chest.

He slowly came in and sat down at the other end of the couch. "Cat," he whispered. I ignored him.

"Cat, look at me."

I was really trying not to cry, and I couldn't look at him. "I'm sorry, Kirin. I'm not ready for this."

"Cat."

I turned then to face him, and saw kindness, compassion, and care in his eyes, a slight smile on his mouth. "Cat, I'm not in the habit of taking advantage of girls, and I'm sorry if I frightened you. Please forgive me."

I opened my mouth to speak, and quickly shut it again. I struggled to find the words to properly express what I was feeling. Softly, I said, "I...I'm not frightened of you."

He scooted closer. "Listen, Cat. I don't know what's going on here, and you can tell me if I'm alone in this, but..." He paused. "I feel like there's something here." He rushed on. "I know that sounds cheesy, and the circumstances are a little unusual, but tell me if I'm wrong, and I'll step away, and when the roads are clear, we'll just go our separate ways."

My lack of a disagreement urged him on, and he slid another inch closer. A grin formed on his face. "If I'm right, then let's get to know each other and see what happens."

"This doesn't make any sense to me."

He laughed, "Yeah, no shit!"

"I *just* got out of a relationship."

"I don't know what to tell you, Cat."

"Doesn't that worry you?"

He scooted the last few inches so that my knees were up against his middle, "Oh, Kitty Cat, if I thought you were still pining for that guy, I never would have kissed you. I'm not worried."

He pulled me towards him so that I could wrap my arms around him. I laid my head on his chest, and he cradled me close.

"You aren't alone in this," I whispered into his chest.

"Well then, let's see how this goes."

"I don't know the first thing about running my own business." I was pacing back and forth in front of the fireplace.

Stopping abruptly, I turned to Kirin, who was laying on the couch. Two throw pillows were propped behind his head at one end, and his ankles were crossed at the other. He was tall, an inch or so over 6 feet, and seeing him laid out like that was distracting me. He had been jotting down notes while I talked.

"What do you mean?" he asked rhetorically. "You've been doing it for years."

"No, I rely on other people."

"Exactly...running a business. Who do you rely on?"

All the faces of the people who had been part of my team flashed through my mind, and I continued my pacing, rattling them off as I walked. "I had an assistant, we had a scheduler, an accountant, a lawyer, and a junior designer."

"Now, tell me all the clients you brought on." His pen was poised, ready to write.

"Why?"

Slowly, he drawled, "You want to go after them."

"You mean, steal them back?"

"That's exactly what I mean, Cat. You brought them on, and you said yourself, the kid they gave your accounts to is useless."

I smirked and said sheepishly, "I didn't exactly say he was useless. I said he was the nephew of the owner, so I don't even really know what he can do."

"Regardless, he stepped into something you built. Don't doubt yourself. You can turn this around and make it something really good for you, make your own rules, and run your own business. Be a shark, Cat!"

His enthusiasm had prompted him to sit up straight, and he was looking at me intently. Giddiness bubbled up inside me, and I thought that maybe I could actually do this.

"Now, again, tell me all the clients you brought on."

I rattled off all the accounts we had already talked about, plus a few smaller accounts that I knew would definitely come with me.

"Ok, now, after the holidays, you start calling them."

"Do you think I should call them today?"

"No. You should not call them today. Get your business plan in place, think about the people you need on your team, and then go meet with the clients in person."

He looked so purposeful—intent on his mission to help me. I sauntered over to him, feeling bold, and stood directly in front of him.

Looking up at me with a glint in his eye, he put the pad of paper on the floor and reached up to grab my hips. "What are you doing?" he asked.

"You look so focused and sexy, I thought I might kiss you."

"By all means, go right ahead."

Lowering myself to his lap, I straddled him, wrapping my arms around his neck and leaning in to kiss him. His

124

mouth maneuvered expertly across mine, and I briefly thought that I could just go on kissing him forever. He pulled back and started kissing the side of my neck, pulling the collar of my shirt out of the way, so he could kiss across my collar bone.

"See, I told you. A distraction," he whispered huskily against my skin and then unceremoniously flipped me to the couch, leaned over, and kissed me hard.

I lay on my back, grinning up at him.

He leaned over and kissed me again. "What a nice Christmas." Then he stood abruptly, picked up the notepad, and handed it to me. "Now, make a plan."

I watched as he bolted up the stairs, returning a minute later with his laptop.

He settled in the recliner, and we sat quietly together for the afternoon, working and watching the snow fall from the branches. He was writing and reading, and I was drafting out a business plan, pausing every now and then to ask for guidance and advice.

Late in the afternoon, I finally put the notepad down, crossed my legs underneath me on the couch, and stared at him curiously. After a moment, he looked up at me over   his glasses and said, "Yes?"

I smiled and started talking to him. "Is there anything you want to tell me about yourself?"

He removed his glasses and smiled back at me. "What do you want to know?"

Sitting up a little straighter, I said, "I don't know, anything. What's your favorite food?"

"Fish Tacos."

"Oh, yum! I can make those."

"Yes, but can you make them like they do in Southern California?"

"Red cabbage? Ranch dressing?"

"Don't forget the Sriracha."

"Of course not!"

We were grinning across the room at each other.

"Favorite sport?"

"To watch, or play?"

"Both."

"To watch, I'd say soccer, but only pee-wee soccer because that is what my nephews play."

"Oh, you just shared something I didn't ask for. Excellent, you're finally opening up."

Laughing, he said, "Ok, your turn."

"Oh, no, you can't just drop that tidbit of information and not continue. How many nephews?"

"Three. And two nieces."

His mention of nieces made me feel a little sad, and I missed my sister.

I sat, quietly reflective in my own thoughts of family, until he prompted me out of my reverie.

"Hey, where'd you go?"

"Just thinking about my family, and how I ended up here."

"Care to share?"

"My musings?"

"Yes."

Waiting a moment, I briefly wondered how open I should be, how vulnerable I wanted to make myself to him. This was an unusual situation, so I just jumped right in.

"I've been so busy building my career, I haven't really thought about just *being* with someone. Sam and I just, well, I already told you. But now...now it feels like it didn't even happened, like we were never important to each other. It seems so superficial now. If everything looked perfect, then it was, right? The perfect job, the perfect boyfriend, car, house, whatever. It just seems really irrelevant now. Nothing has felt more real to me— that I can remember—than right now." I ended on a rush, disbelieving that I had actually said all that. I waited while he watched me, a grin growing on his face. Nervously, I continued, "And now, this is where you say something really profound, and help me not feel so silly." His grin was wide on his face, as he lowered the foot rest on his recliner and came to stand in front of me, hands resting on the back of the couch, bracketing me in place.

I put my head back so I could look up at him.

"Cat, it doesn't seem important to you now, because it isn't. The core of who we are, the way we treat people, how we spend our time together? That's what's important. The external stuff? It's just stuff. Hanging out with you, even if that's the only thing we do today, is better than anything I could have dreamt up, or imagined, or planned."

"Oh, my! Did you write that?" My mouth watered, and I wanted to kiss him. I didn't have to wait long.

A devilish grin crossed his face. "It was good, wasn't it?" He dropped a kiss to my forehead, and then gave me a hard kiss on my mouth. "I'm gonna start dinner." And he kissed me again.

I could hear pots and pans being banged around in the kitchen, so I joined him to see if I could help. Sitting on a barstool at the counter, I watched as he put a pot of water on the stove to boil.

Chicken was cooking in a skillet, and I watched as he added some rosemary and olive oil.

"Can I help?"

"Do you want to put the bread in the oven and pour us some wine?"

"I can do that." I hopped off the barstool and wrapped the bread in tinfoil, placing it in the center of the pre-heated oven.

He handed me a wine opener, and I opened a bottle of the local cabernet, filling two very large glasses.

Dubiously, he watched as I took a generous drink.

"Long day," I said sardonically.

He laughed, and went back to turning the chicken.

"Can I share with you what I have for a business plan?"

Smiling at me over his shoulder, he said, "I would love to hear your business plan."

As he cooked, I read my drafted plan to him, and I saw him nod, and pause, and then nod again, as if he was really processing what I was sharing with him. He effortlessly moved from the stove to the sink to drain the pasta, and then tossed in the chicken and some sun-dried tomatoes.

I set the table for two and lit the candle that was in the center, its pine tree scent infusing the room.

Carrying over the bowl of pasta and two smaller bowls for each of us, he placed the bowls on the table, and then pulled a chair out for me to sit. He scooted me in before returning to the kitchen for the bread.

When he finally sat down, I raised my wine glass to him in a toast. "To being snowed in."

"May it always happen with your favorite person." He clinked his glass against mine.

His response made me giggle, and this time, I took a smaller sip.

After serving us each a bowl-full of the steaming noodles, he reached for his phone in his back pocket, and I watched as he tapped on it a few times, and then set it on the table next to him. Softly, Christmas music started to play on the house stereo system, and my eyes opened wider in awe.

"How did you discover that?"

"Nick told me they had blue-tooth."

"Well, thank you. The music is perfect." I smiled at him, and we ate our dinner in comfortable companionship, talking more about Laguna Beach and how quaint and perfect it is.

"You should come visit."

His stare was unwavering, and I found myself nodding, not able to break away from his emerald gaze. "I'd like that."

He nodded affirmatively and picked up his fork to finish eating.

When we were both finished, I cleared our dishes, and he watched as I washed them, leaning back in his chair, popping Hershey's kisses in his mouth and sipping his wine.

"Do you know how to play cribbage?"

I finished the dishes, wiped down the counter and hung the towel over the faucet to dry. "I don't. Is it a card game?"

"Yeah. C'mon, I'll teach you."

We played for almost an hour, drinking our wine and laughing every time I beat him.

"Beginner's luck."

"Yeah, right. You just aren't very good."

I scooped up the cards to start another game, and he put his hand out to softly push my hand, and the cards, back to the table. My smile dropped, and I looked up at his now-serious face.

"Cat, I need to tell you something, and I want you to just listen, okay?"

"Okay." Warily, I sat back and waited.

"I am…" He looked like he was going to tell me one thing, and then seemed to shift to another. "I am incredibly attracted to you. I don't know how the gods, or fates, or goddesses—or whatever you want to call them—brought us here together, but I'm so grateful that they did." He paused and took a deep breath. Letting it out slowly, he started again. "I want to make love with you, but I don't want you to feel pressured, or anxious, or obligated. I just wanted you to know. And if you want that too, then you just let me know—and if you aren't sure, that's ok too. But I wanted you to know how I feel."

My breath sped up a little at his honesty and straightforwardness. "Thank you. I don't know how I feel right now. I want to be near you, and maybe sleep with you—and by that, I mean actual sleep." He laughed as I rushed out the words.

"I know what you meant." He rose from the table and reached for my hand. "C'mon."

He turned off the kitchen and dining room lights and dropped my hand to plug in the Christmas tree.

Guiding me over to the couch, he lay down and pulled me to him, tucking me alongside him with my back against the couch. I curled into him, my leg thrown over his leg, and he cradled me against him. We lay like that for what seemed like forever, listening to the soft Christmas music and watching the lights on the tree sparkle on the glass windows. My head was on his chest, my arm draped across his middle. I could hear his heart beating, and as I faded off to sleep, I thought that this felt like the safest place in the world.

10

"Good morning, Cat."

I rolled my ankles and stretched, pointing my toes and reaching my arms high above my head. Sometime during the night, Kirin had rolled out from underneath me and placed a blanket over me, tucking me in so that I stayed warm without him.

Opening my eyes lazily, I spotted him perched on the side of the couch, smiling adoringly down at me.

"Good morning." I smiled back at him, pulling the blanket up higher to keep my neck warm. "It's freezing in here."

"I'll make a fire in a minute. Coffee's ready. Do you want some?" I nodded and he patted my hip as he stood.

"What are we going to do today?" I called after him.

Coming back around the corner, he handed a mug of hot coffee to me and sat down again on the couch.

"Am I your social coordinator now, too? Is that role in your business plan?"

I gave him my best sexy smile. "I think I could find a suitable service role for you in my plan."

He reached under the blanket and seductively ran his hand up the side of my thigh. Holy freaking Mary! If I had any doubts about making love to him last night, they just completely evaporated— poof! I was all-in this morning.

Firmly, he squeezed my hip and let his hand drop down to my bottom. My breath hitched, eyes glittering mischievously. He lowered his head to the crook of my neck, his lips barely grazing my skin, and said, "Just because you're the boss, that doesn't mean I can't handle you."

Heat rushed through my body; I put my head back, felt my legs spread, and   noticed my hand start to drop my coffee.

He jolted up, laughing, just in time to catch my mug from spilling over. "You need to pay attention."

"You're mean!"

"You are adorable."

I sat back up, pulling my knees to my chest, partly for warmth, and partly because I was no longer immune to him.

I watched as he got down on his haunches to start the fire, admiring the view of his broad back. He glanced at me over his shoulder, a knowing smile on his face, and I took a sip of my coffee, grinning at him.

"I went out this morning to check the roads, and they are still pretty deep with snow. I don't think your little car would make it out."

"Darn." I snapped my fingers.

I heard him laugh as he blew on the kindling.

"Since its Christmas Eve, I think we should have a date."

"What do you mean, a date? We're already stuck here." I took another sip of my coffee.

He stood, the fire now a soft glow behind him.

"Cat, this might be an unusual situation, but I would still like to take you on a date tonight."

Butterflies flitted in my stomach. I drawled, "Okay. What do you have in mind?"

"How would you usually get ready for any other date?"

Quickly, I catalogued the clothes I'd brought with me. I didn't have anything remotely sexy. Did I even pack any of my good makeup?

When I didn't immediately respond, he said, "You don't have to be fancy. I just want to treat you like I would if we were going on a real date. Don't think too hard about it, Cat."

I rushed on to correct him, "I'm not. I was just thinking about what I have to wear."

"Feel free to come out naked, if that's how you want to start the evening." He sounded half-serious, and I threw a pillow at him.

We spent a lazy day together, reading and napping. Around four that afternoon, he stood and said he was going to head upstairs to shower and change.

Nervously, I asked him what he wanted me to do.

"Why don't you do the same? Take your time. I'll start something for dinner.

Come out when you're ready." Leaning over me, he pressed his lips softly to mine, gently sucking on first my top lip, and then the bottom, reaching out with his tongue to the seam of my lips and caressing me. I sighed, heard a soft moan, and realized it was me.

Gently, he pulled back, his hand caressing my cheek, and I raised my fingertips to my still wet mouth, my eyes to his.

"See you in a bit," he whispered, and gave me another quick kiss on the forehead, breathing in the scent of me.

I took my time in the shower, using a coconut body wash and a champagne toast shampoo that I found in the bathroom cabinet. Thank goodness I packed a razor and some lotion.

There was a hair dryer under the sink, and a curling iron that looked like it was from the 90's. Hair-spray burn marks charred the barrel. I used it anyway.

My makeup was simple. I hadn't packed any of my night-out makeup, so I went with tinted moisturizer, mascara, and some root beer flavored Chapstick.

Wrapped in a towel, I slowly opened the bathroom door and peeked out into the hall to see if he was there. Not seeing him, I quickly dashed from the bathroom to my bedroom and shut the door behind me. My attempted stealth made me giggle, and I sat down on the edge of the bed to catch my breath.

Staring towards the closet, I noticed something glittering in the corner. I tilted my head to see if I'd imagined it. I hadn't: something with sequins was hanging in the back.

I slowly stood, and, reaching in to the closet, I pulled out a short, low-cut, black sequined...dress? I wasn't sure if it was supposed to be a tunic for a tall person or a dress for a short person. Regardless, it was super sexy, and I ran my hands over the sequins wistfully.

Could I wear this tonight? I would have to ask Shaye about this dress after the holidays.

Unwrapping my towel, I dressed in my bra and underwear and slid the dress over my head. Oops! This wasn't going to work. My breast size rarely allowed me to go without a bra, but the front of this dress was so low, I wouldn't be able to wear one.

I pulled the dress off, removed my bra, and then slipped the dress back on. Holy cow! The front conformed beautifully to my breasts, supporting them even without the bra, and I felt free. This was a sex dress, for sure!

My shoe options consisted of leather boots, UGGS, and the shoes I wore up here. Barefoot it was. I slid a silver bracelet on my wrist, and kept my standard diamond studs in my ears.

Through the door, I heard Christmas music playing. The cabin was toasty warm from the fire Kirin had kept burning all day, and I took a deep breath to calm my nerves before opening the bedroom door.

Tentatively, I walked out into the living room. Kirin was standing in the center of the room, staring out into the forest through the windows. My chest felt heavy, and I couldn't breathe. His charcoal slim-fit trousers hugged his thighs, tapering to low-cut lace-up chukka boots. I could see his reflection in the glass, and when he finally saw me reflected behind him, he turned and stared.

"Cat." His voice was filled with reverence, and I almost wept with longing for him.

A white T-shirt peeked out from behind his gray quarter-zip pullover sweater, and I wanted to rush into his arms and squeeze him.

Instead, I stood and waited, not able to speak.

"I...I..." He stuttered, and glanced down at my chest, his eyes roving down to my toes and back up to my face. "I don't even...I can't even." He dropped his chin to his chest and laughed. "Cat, I can't even speak."

I shifted from one foot to the other, flirting with him. "Do I look okay?"

My teasing tone relaxed us both, and he took a step forward, enveloping me in a hug, burying his face in my neck, and twirling me around. "You look wretched. I can't bear to look at you."

When my feet were firmly planted back on the ground, he cradled my face in his hands and kissed me quickly, talking with his lips pressed against mine. "I'm so glad it snowed."

I held onto his wrists for balance.

Releasing me, he reached down to the coffee table and grabbed a small package—wrapped in brown paper from the grocery store bag. He had drawn a bow on it with a crayon.

"For you." He handed me the present.

"How could you possibly have gotten me a gift?"

"At the store the other day. I was going to give it to you when you left the next day, but—well, here we are."

I unwrapped it gently and pulled out a ferry boat keychain with the inscription, *Lopez Island*. I tried to stop the tears that threatened to fall, but I couldn't.

Wrapping my arms tightly around him, I rested my cheek against his chest. "Thank you. This is the most perfect gift I've ever received. Thank you."

His arms engulfed me, his chin resting on the top of his head. I heard him whisper,   "You're welcome."

After a moment, he pulled back. "You hungry?"

"Starved."

"Stay right here. We're going to eat here, in front of the tree."

His little boy enthusiasm made me laugh, and I did my best to sit on the plush rug without flashing him or falling out of my top.

He returned carrying two plates, which he set down on the coffee table, and then ran back into the kitchen for a bottle of wine and two glasses.

He had cooked a fresh salmon with a sprig of dill, red potatoes, and asparagus.

"This is beautiful! I guess you were planning on staying here awhile."

Wariness flashed in his eyes, but it was gone before I could question it.

Raising my glass to his, I toasted, "To my best Christmas ever."

"Cheers."

We ate in silence for a moment, each of us enjoying the flavor of the fresh salmon and the serenity of the evening.

After a while, I asked him what he would be doing tonight if he wasn't here.

Setting his fork down on his plate, he said. "I would be with my family at my parents' house—most likely chasing the little hellions around, and feeding them

144

tons of sugar so that they would keep my brothers and sisters-in-law awake."

His answer made me laugh. "Do you miss them?"

Taking a sip of his wine, he paused before responding. "In general? Nope. I see them all the time. Tonight? Definitely not."

His look had turned tender, and I felt his emerald stare. My appetite suddenly gone, I slowly put my fork down on my plate and stared heatedly back at him.

Like a hunter, he reached for my ankles, pulling them out from under me. The dress was so short, I was sure he could see my panties as he pulled me towards him, and I didn't care. The movement forced me backwards, and I braced my arms behind me.

I was now spread out in front of him, watching as his hands ran over my calves, caressing me.

"Lie back," he whispered seductively.

Slowly, I lowered myself to my elbows, never taking my eyes off him. He was on his knees between my spread legs, kissing his way up my calves and thighs.

His beard tickled the soft skin of my inner thighs, and I closed my eyes in ecstasy.

His hands pushed at the dress, and I lifted my bottom so he could shove it up over my hips as I lay back on the rug. Moving the dress higher and higher up my body, he placed soft kisses over every inch of skin he revealed. Under the fabric, his hands rubbed the underside of my breasts, and I started to moan beneath him.

Finally, he raised the dress the last couple of inches, and my breasts sprang free. He took one of my nipples in his mouth, and I moaned out loud, throwing my head back in pleasure and arching my back.

Frantically, I tried to remove the rest of the dress myself so I could get my body closer to him. It came up over my head chaotically, and his mouth crashed down on mine. I wrapped my legs around his waist and pulled his heavy weight down on top of me.

I tried to remove his sweater, and he grabbed both of my wrists, raising them above my head. Panting, my eyes focused, and I realized he had stopped.

146

"Why are you stopping?"

He laughed. "I'm not stopping. I'm just looking at you."

"Can you look later? I'm a little worked up."

He sat back from me, stood up, and reached out a hand to help me up.

Eyeing him warily, I reached for his hand, and he walked me to the foot of the stairs.

Looking up, I saw that he had hung a mistletoe from an exposed beam.

Standing in front of him, wearing nothing but my panties, I said, "Did you buy that the other day too?"

He grinned like he had done something incredibly important. "I did."

"Hopeful?"

He thought for a moment. "Optimistic."

I smiled up at him, and he continued seriously, "It's up to you, Cat."

I bit my lower lip, making him wait a moment, and then I reached my arms around his neck and raised my mouth to kiss him.

Lifting me up off the floor, he carried me up the stairs.

11

We spent most of Christmas Day in bed. Periodically, one of us would get up to bring food back from the kitchen, but for the most part, we made a camp in the Master Bedroom.

The room was large and cozy, with dark brown walls, luxurious carpet, a four-poster bed that gave it a rustic, masculine feel, and a down comforter that kept us snuggly and warm. Like a loft, it was open to the living room, and I could see out into the forest through the floor-to-ceiling windows.

I was envious that he had been sleeping up here in this massive king-size bed, with its fluffy down mattress, and I told him so late that night.

"You do know I'm not moving back downstairs?" I said as I snuggled my bottom up against his middle, and he spooned behind me.

Nuzzling my neck, he mumbled, "That was my plan all along."

We fell asleep, waking in the middle of the afternoon to make love again, slowly and sweetly.

On one of his trips downstairs that day, he made a fire to warm the cabin, and brought back a deck of cards and some DVD's he found in the second back bedroom.

"We have 'It's a Wonderful Life,' or 'Elf.' Which do you prefer?"

Being with him was so easy and comfortable.

"Both." I smiled up at him. This was the best Christmas I could ever remember.

That night, we settled in bed, the flames from the fire making shadows on the cabin walls. I slept peacefully and soundly wrapped in his arms, listening to the melting snow falling from the branches of the trees onto the metal roof.

In the morning, the day after Christmas, we were woken by the sounds of a large diesel truck rumbling up the gravel driveway.

Kirin untangled himself from me, kissed me quickly, and rolled out of bed.

I watched appreciatively as he pulled on a pair of plaid flannel pajama bottoms and a sweatshirt.

"Wicked woman." He grinned when he noticed my lascivious stare.

I giggled and buried myself back under the covers.

The catwalk creaked as he walked across it, and I heard his feet pad down the stairs, and then the front door open.

Muffled voices went back and forth, and a few moments later, Kirin came bounding up the stairs, and jumped on top of me, kissing me and nuzzling me like a dog.

"Stop! What are you doing?" I was laughing and couldn't catch a breath.

He finally stopped, crawled under the covers, and curled himself around me.

"The roads are clear, and he's going to plow and sand the driveway." It occurred to me that I was free to leave.

I pulled my head back so that I could see him. I stared at him pensively, waiting for him to continue. He put his bottom lip out in a pout, and my heart thundered in my chest. I prayed he

150

wouldn't say something like, 'nice knowing ya.'

He raised himself up on one elbow and looked down at me. "When were you originally planning on heading home?"

"Sometime between the twenty-eighth and thirtieth. I have a New Year's Eve party to attend."

Our conversation was wary, each of us gauging how much of our feelings to share, knowing that we were free to go. Our eyes were trying to say to each other what we were afraid to say with words.

He spoke first, his thoughts coming out in a rush. "Stay with me, Cat. Stay until the New Year. Just until the New Year, and then you can go. I don't want you to go."

My grin grew, and my heart lightened. "What could we possibly do for all those days?"

He pulled me back underneath him and said, "I think we can probably get creative."

The truck engine interrupted our mood, and the distraction made it difficult to continue with our "creativity."

Rolling back off me and sitting up in bed, he looked over his shoulder at me, lying all tousled against the pillow. "Want to go into town? Get some lunch?"

"No, I don't want to leave the house," I pouted sullenly.

He stepped out of bed, turned, and reached under the covers to grab my ankles. "C'mon, I can't stay holed up here one day longer."

He pulled me toward the edge of the bed, and I laughed and tried to kick free. "Noooo."

Finally, he had pulled me close enough to pat my bottom. Laughing, he said, "Yes! Go take a shower. I'll meet you downstairs."

I grudgingly went back downstairs to my room and realized how small it really was. I couldn't wait to get back upstairs and sleep with him tonight.

An hour later, I met him on the back porch where he was waiting, bundled up in his down parka and boots.

He held his hand out to me and grinned. "I'll drive."

"Are you afraid of my driving?"

"No, it just looks like fun. C'mon, hand 'em over." He wiggled his fingers at me, and I placed the keys in the palm of his hand.

"Okay." I said dubiously, and then rushed on. "But be careful."

He opened the passenger door and held it for me as I stepped in and buckled up.

His driving was safe and calm, and I realized how nice it was to have someone else do the driving.

He made a comment about making sure I had the car cleaned when I got back to Seattle. "All the salt and gravel will destroy the undercarriage of your car."

The town was still quiet as we drove into the main village, parking in front of the pizza restaurant. Snow berms lined the streets, and flakes of snow blew off the branches of the trees, fluttering to the ground around us as we stepped out of the car.

It appeared we weren't the only ones who had cabin fever—I counted six other cars in the parking lot.

We entered the restaurant, and a woman behind the counter tossing pizza dough gave us a quick look, and then greeted us.

"Hey, Kirin, how you doing? Did you survive the snow?"

"I did, thanks for asking. This is Cat, a friend of Shaye's." He introduced me, and a puzzled look crossed her face.

She glanced quickly between the two of us, and then she smiled graciously. "Welcome. I'm Amy. It's nice to meet you."

Quickly looking back to Kirin, she told us to take a seat anywhere, and someone would be right with us.

This was a very cozy restaurant, small and inviting, with only a few tables toward the back, and one near the front for larger parties. Four bar stools were at the front counter for those who wanted to dine alone, or just watch the pizzas being baked in the brick oven.

Paprika-colored walls, textured in a stucco style, created an intimate environment, and the checkered tablecloths reminded me of an Italian café. I could imagine it would be a very romantic place for dinner, with the candles on each table lit.

We hung our coats on a rack near the front door, and after we were seated, a waitress brought us menus and took our drink order. Kirin ordered coffee, me, a coke.

When she returned with our drinks, Kirin looked questioningly at me, "BBQ Chicken, red onions, mozzarella, and gorgonzola?"

I looked up at the waitress. "Sounds perfect!"

Kirin reached across the table and took my hands in his. "When are you coming to California?"

I blinked, caught off guard. My surprise must have shown because he laughed and continued on. "No rush, but I would like you to come visit."

His eyes flitted to someone who had just walked in, and he pulled his hands out of mine, raised his eyes, and waved at the person. I turned in my chair and saw a very broad man in a suit sitting at the counter, ordering a pizza to go.

When he finished ordering, the man wandered over to us, and Kirin stood to greet him. "Ethan, good to see you!"

They shook hands, and then he introduced us. "Ethan Archer, this is Caitlyn Darling, a friend of Shaye's. She goes by Cat."

"Cat, nice to meet you. Are you staying in their house while they're in Hawaii?"

I glanced quickly at Kirin, and he jumped in to save me. "Yes. Yes, she is."

"Nice. Well, it's nice to meet you."

Turning his attention back to Kirin, he crossed his arms and his brows furrowed over his eyes. "Hey, any word on that girl? Did they find her yet?"

Kirin looked a little awkward, and his eyes flitted to mine. "No, not yet, but hopefully soon."

The air was charged between the three of us, and I suddenly felt uncomfortable, as if I was missing something.

Ethan withdrew from the conversation, as if he had just said something he shouldn't have, and put a smile back on his face. "Well, I'll let the two of you get back to your lunch." They shook hands again, and Ethan acknowledged me again as he retreated back to the counter.

Kirin sat back down, and I heard Ethan tell Amy he would be back in twenty minutes for the pizza.

We sat in silence for a few minutes before I finally asked who the girl was.

He adjusted himself a little awkwardly in the chair. "A girl from Laguna Beach went missing. Haven't found her yet." He pulled his lips in between his teeth, and then popped them back out.

"How does Ethan know about her?" I was getting a sinking feeling in my stomach that he wasn't telling me everything.

Just then, our lunch arrived, and Kirin ignored my question. I picked at my slice while Kirin ate in silence.

I felt tension radiating off of him, and the wariness I'd felt a few days ago came flooding back. I realized that I didn't actually know that much about him, and that I'd rushed into this...whatever it was...with less caution than I probably should have. I have never been very impulsive. But then again, this entire trip was out of character for me.

He paid the bill, and I met him outside at the car.

We rode home in silence, and I saw him tapping his fingers nervously on his legs, lost in thought. I turned to stare out

157

the window, watching the trees with bare winter branches and the still-frozen snow on the ground as we passed them by.

All I could think about was that I really didn't want to go back to that place where my heart was broken. What I had with Kirin felt so real. Despite my impulsivity, being with him felt more real than anything had in a long time. I felt numb at the possibility of it all falling apart.

When we reached the house, I stepped out of the car before he had even turned off the ignition.

"Cat, are you ok?" he called after me as I climbed the back steps.

"Yeah, I'm fine, I think I just want to lay down for a while. Read a book, maybe."

He followed me into the house and approached me as he might a rabid dog. He took me slowly in his arms, and I had difficulty looking at him. He moved his head back and forth to try to catch my eyes, and then leaned in to kiss the side of my neck.

I felt tears welling up, and I didn't know why. I closed my eyes and let him kiss me.

I heard him speak softly in my ear. "Ok, I'll leave you to rest. I'm gonna go upstairs and work for a bit."

I stepped back and nodded at him, a hesitant smile on my face.

Taking a Nora Roberts novel from the bookcase, I laid down on the couch, covered myself with a blanket, and stared at the pages, not really seeing the words. I must have fallen asleep because I woke to the sound of a truck pulling into the driveway.

I got up to meet whoever had arrived, opening the back door and crossing my arms to ward off the cold.

A very flamboyant man in a purple velvet coat and lavender skinny jeans stepped out of an old Ford pickup truck. He brushed himself off as if to remove the stigma of driving such an old vehicle.

"Can I help you?"

"I'm here for Alex. Get him, would you? We need to go."

My head snapped back. What a rude human being. "I'm sorry, I think you might have the wrong house."

He started climbing the steps and laughed at me. "No, darling, I don't think so. I dropped him off here."

I stepped in front of him to prevent him from getting into the house, just as I heard Kirin bounding down the stairs.

"Cat."

I turned to see Kirin standing behind me, a look of regret on his face.

"Thank God! You're still here. We need to go!" The fancy man looked at me, as if he had just eaten something bitter. "And call off your little island girl here so that I can get into the house."

I stepped aside, shocked and confused.

He walked passed me, talking almost to himself. "Do you know how much trouble I've had trying to get here? This weather has been just awful."

I stalked after him. "I'm not an island girl."

He looked at Kirin and said, "Another crazy one?"

"What are you doing here, James?"

"They found the girl. She's been arrested, and they have her in custody."

"I'm confused. What's going on?" I looked back and forth between the two of them.

160

"Cat, I need to talk to you." Kirin grabbed my elbow and gently-but firmly steered me into the hall.

I stood against the wall. "Who is that guy?"

"His name is James. He's my assistant." Kirin rubbed his palms across his face, put them on his hips, and looked heavenward.

James took that moment to shout from the dining room, "You need to be in court Monday. Can you please get your things? I would like to get off this rock before dark."

I pulled my head back so that I could focus on him more clearly, and all the little dominoes in my head started clicking into place—memories of all the news stories I'd half paid attention to finally giving me the reason he was here.

In shock, I put my right hand to my mouth and my left hand on my bicep. "Oh. My. God. You're Alexander Stone. The actor. That story. The girl—she was stalking you." My words were coming out broken, fragmented.

I dropped to the third step on the stairs, and repeated. "Oh my God. Oh my God. She tried to kill you."

I stood back up abruptly and pushed him, poking my finger to his chest, shouting—almost accusingly— "You're Alexander Stone!   "

"Cat, listen to me. I wanted to tell you."

I ran into the bedroom and slammed the door shut. I sat down on the bed, wishing he would come in, hoping he wouldn't.

Kirin, or Alex—whatever his name was—said through the door, "Cat, I'm not leaving until you come out."

I stood from the bed and opened the door. "I'm so embarrassed that I didn't know who you were."

"I'm glad you didn't know."

"Wow, this must have been a nice little distraction for you, and I made it easy, didn't I? The poor, sad little broken-hearted girl you so easily seduced? What a fun little game to help you pass the time!"

Kirin braced his hands against the door-jamb and said emphatically, in response to my tirade, "No!"

His assistant shouted again from the other room. "Alex! We need to go! The plane is waiting, and I've got to get rid of that awful truck and get the stench of it off of me."

I didn't have the energy for this. I just wanted to go home. "Please, just leave."

"This isn't over. I have to go, but we aren't through."

His pesky assistant came around the corner. "Alex, as quaint as this is, and as lovely as I am sure this was, it's time to go."

Kirin looked at me with sadness, regret, and despondency all wrapped up in one. I stared back vacantly. He slowly retreated, and I heard him run up the stairs to gather his things.

I retreated back into the room, curled up on my side on the bed, and stared out the window. The snow looked so pure, so fresh. It was in direct opposition to the sad feelings swirling around in my heart.

James appeared in my doorway, holding his cell phone. "Excuse me, I'm having horrible reception up here. Do you know what I need to do?"

I stood from the bed, stalked to the bedroom door, and shut it in his face.

"Rude!" he intoned from the other side of the door. Then he shouted up the stairs, "Alex, I'm waiting outside."

A few minutes later, I heard Kirin come down the stairs. He stopped outside the bedroom door.

"Cat, I'm sorry I didn't tell you," he whispered through the door. "I'm sorry you had to find out like this. I didn't know who you were when you got here—I wasn't sure I could trust you. I was going to tell you, but there just didn't seem to be a right time."

I opened the door. He had been leaning his forehead on the door, and he nearly fell in on me.

"Kirin. Alex. Whoever you are. It doesn't matter. I'm going back to my world. You're going back to yours. So, good meeting you. Have a nice life."

"It's not ending this way."

"Yes, it is."

"I'm going to call you!"

I nodded and twisted up my face, realizing he didn't even have my number.

This guy was a piece of work, and I'd been so easy for him.

He swooped in and kissed me hard, and retreated before I had a chance to respond.

He grabbed my hand. I tried to pull away, but he held on tight. "I will call you!"

I pulled hard on my fingers until he released them. Stepping back, I looked him in the eye. "Good-bye, Alex."

12

The following Monday, I was sitting on my couch, watching the entertainment channel, waiting for news on Kirin, or Alex, or whoever he was. I didn't even know what I was supposed to call him anymore.

I'd left the island the day after Kirin left.

The day he left, I'd quietly packed up my things and contacted the name of the cleaning service that Shaye had put on her original email to me.

I'd locked myself in the downstairs bedroom and slept fitfully. The house was lonely and a little bit scary, and I hadn't realized how safe I'd felt with him there until he wasn't.

My roommate Erin had come home late the night before from her week with her parents, and now I was waiting for her to get home from work.

She came through the front door, saw me, squealed, and sat down next to me on the couch, enveloping me in a big hug.

"How was your Christmas? I missed you so much! I almost got on a boat and came over, but then Perry showed up at my parents' house and blew that idea right out of the water." She looked smitten and was glowing.

"Wow! Seriously?" We hadn't talked all week, and I wasn't sure how much I wanted to share about meeting Kirin. It was bad enough that I was sitting here watching a pop-culture show hoping to see him.

We were interrupted by the TV news announcer. "Actor and Academy Award-winning screenwriter Alexander Stone appeared in court today to testify on the recent stalking and attempted murder case. Stone, made famous after his Oscar for his screenplay adaptation of 'To Live and Breathe,' was the victim of a real-life Annette, the main character of the film, who stalks and kills Hollywood men who resemble her father."

Erin was transfixed to the television. "Have you been following this? So scary. Poor guy, responded on Twitter to some random comment, and the next thing you know, he's being stalked in restaurants and at his gym. This girl followed him everywhere." Her words were tumbling out of her mouth, and I only half heard her.

Kirin was on the screen, and his lovely face was all I could focus on. His hair was cut short, and he had shaved his beard. God, that mouth... His face was so chiseled without the facial hair, and even though I couldn't see his eyes, I knew they were emerald green, and would be bright against his tanned face. His charcoal gray tailor-made suit accentuated every muscle I knew so well, and the white shirt and burgundy striped tie lay flat against a lean, cut stomach. I felt my heart squeeze and had to hold back tears. This was Kirin. A very polished Kirin, but I knew him. I liked the Kirin from the island better, but I knew that wasn't real.

Erin's voice was still droning on, and I finally came back from my swooning. "...and apparently, she snuck

168

into his house in Laguna Beach over Thanksgiving weekend and crawled into bed with him. When he tried to get away from her, she pulled a gun on him, going on about how her father had abused her, and how all of them must die. He tried to tackle her, but she escaped over his balcony, and there has been a huge hunt for her since. It's been just crazy!" She paused for a breath, and then swooned. "Christ, he is so freaking hot!"

I silently agreed, turned back to the TV, and let out a heavy sigh.

"I'm so sorry. I asked you how your week was, and then I got completely distracted by a sexy thing on the TV. How are you?"

"I'm good. It was good. It snowed and was really beautiful. It was relaxing and peaceful and beautiful."

She stared at me, her brow furrowed, and then slowly said, "Okay."

"And that's it."

"Uhm. Those are all lovely adjectives, but something isn't right. You were all hell-bent on getting out of here, and now..." She wiggled her finger in the air, making circles around me. "And now, this. This is a bland version of you."

I took a deep breath, pulled a pillow to my chest, and then let out all the air I was holding, puffing out my cheeks. "You may not believe me."

"Try me." She sat up straighter on the couch and gave me her full attention.

"Okay, but it's really quite a story."

"Enough! Talk!" She raised her eyebrows at me and pushed her forehead forward, urging me to tell her.

"Okay, well, I got to the house really late, and there was someone already there. He tackled me to the ground and thought I was an intruder, which makes perfect sense now—but anyway, we realized the mix-up the next day: that Shaye thought Kirin, I mean Alex," I nodded at the TV to indicate that I meant *that* Alex, "was staying at their house, not their rental cabin, and then by the time I made the decision to leave, we got snowed in, and then he helped me figure out how to start my own business, and we just got really close, and then we had sex, and I totally fell for him, and then his assistant showed up and told Alex it was time to go, and he left, and now I'm back home, alone."

She stared at me shell-shocked, and then busted out laughing. "That is the funniest story I've ever heard. How did you come up with that so quickly? That is fantastic. You should write short stories, Cat."

I sat quietly, staring at her, waiting for her laughter to subside, trying to convey my seriousness.

Realization finally dawned, and she abruptly stopped laughing. "Oh my God! You're serious!" She shook her head. "Cat! Are you serious?"

"Yeah, I'm serious. Apparently, a friend of his is the sister of one of Shaye's husband's employees, Ethan Archer."

"Oh my God! Skylar Archer?" She practically jumped up off the couch.

"Erin! Why do you know these people?"

"Why do you not? Seriously, Cat! Skylar Archer is like the new Jennifer Lawrence."

"Well, I *do* know who she is. But really, I don't pay attention to pop culture. I have no idea. I can tell you who won the Super G at the Olympics, but I don't follow Hollywood."

She sat staring at me, dazed. "Wow! I just...wow!"

"Yep." I nodded.

"Wait, what did you call him?"

"Kirin. He said his name was Kirin Anderson."

"Yeah, that makes sense. His name is Kirin Alexander Stone. I don't know where the Anderson came from. It's kind of vanilla, maybe just easy to say off the cuff."

I just shrugged my shoulders, not knowing how to respond to that.

She said again, "Wow!"

"Yeah, you said that."

"I just can't believe this. What are you going to do?"

"Well, I have a New Year's Eve party to attend tomorrow night, and I'm going to try and get some of the clients I brought into the agency to leave Starling Design, and let me represent them."

"No, Cat, I mean what are you going to do about Kirin?"

"Nothing. I'm going to do nothing."

Solemnly, she let the conversation drop, and asked me about my plan to start a business.

"I made a list of all the clients I brought in. Most of them will be at the party, and I intend to share my plan with them, my vision for what I can do for their company."

"How did you get that idea?" she teased me.

"I just figured it out while I was away."

Mockingly, she said, "Uh-huh. I knew something good would happen this week."

"Don't get too excited. I still need to make my pitch and get on their radar. Next week, I intend to start meeting with them, and I'm going to make this business happen."

"That's brilliant, Cat, but isn't the party for your former employer's company?"

"No, the invite came to me. I wasn't uninvited, so I'm going."

We sat silently for a moment, and she stared sadly at me. "Did he say anything before he left?"

I glanced at her briefly, then lowered my eyes to the ground. "He said he would call me."

That got her excited. "See! That's positive."

"Erin, I never gave him my number," I said sardonically.

"Oh."

Her deflated response made me laugh.

She tried again to give me a pep talk. "Sometimes these things work out."

I stood from the couch and turned off the TV, the entertainment news having moved on to a new segment. "I appreciate your positive thoughts, but I'm not putting a whole lot of energy into thinking about it. He may live in Hollywood, but I live in the real world."

She took my cue to change subjects and asked me if I was going to stay for dinner. "Perry is coming over. I can cook for three."

"I'm happy for you, Erin. He seemed like a genuinely nice guy, but no, I think I'll pass tonight. I have a lot to do to get ready for the new business, so I'm going to head upstairs and work. I'll grab a sandwich later."

She watched me walk away, a sad smile on her face. I didn't want her pity. I wanted Kirin.

Sometime in the middle of the night, after I had finalized my strategy, I took myself to bed, prepared for tomorrow.

I took my time getting ready the next evening, making sure I looked polished, elegant, and confident. The girl that brought the clients in couldn't be the same girl to manage the business. They had to trust my business knowledge, not just my design talent.

I washed my hair and dried it straight, then wrapped it in a neat chignon at the base of my neck. Chandelier earrings sparkled in my ears, easily visible with my hair pulled back as it was. My silver lamé mermaid style dress clung to my slim hips and wrapped over one shoulder.

Sitting on the edge of my bed, I was slipping on my black stilettos when I heard a soft knock at my door.

Erin tentatively came in. "Knock, knock." She paused when she saw me. "Oh, Cat, you look stunning."

I stood, grabbed my black fake-fur shrug, and went to hug her. "Thank you. I feel good."

"You're going to nail it tonight. I just know it."

I puffed out my chest a little and raised my chin, giving a haughty pose. "I am."

We both laughed, and then she said, "Seriously, Cat. You're going to be amazing tonight. Go get those clients."

The Olympic Hotel in downtown Seattle is an iconic luxury hotel, with beautiful Georgian architecture and old-world elegance. I drove my own car, since I knew an Uber or a cab would be hard to come by tonight. Besides, I was there for business. I would get in and get out as quickly as possible.

A valet took my car, and I entered the lavish front doors of the hotel. An expansive staircase with wrought-iron railings rose to the second-floor ballroom, where I checked in and was greeted with a flute glass of champagne. I found my name on a seating chart and made my way to my table.

The ballroom was decorated in silver balloons and streamers, and with my silver dress, I almost blended in with the decor.

Placing my shrug on the back of my chair, I looked up and instantly saw my former boss across the room. I gave him a little wave, and I saw his face flush red. He waddled towards me, and I pasted a pleasant smile on my face. Surprisingly, the bitterness and resentment I'd felt for him almost two weeks ago had been replaced with disappointment and apathy.

"Mr. Peterson, lovely to see you."

"Cat, what are you doing here?"

"I was invited."

"No, the invitation was for the company."

"With respect, sir, the invitation was sent to me. There was even a seat reserved in my name. See?" I indicated the place card with my name on it.

His mouth silently opened and closed a few times, making him look like an over-large fish. But eventually he found his voice again. "I don't like this one bit, Cat. You shouldn't be here."

He knew what I was doing. Even better, he knew that I knew, and that made it so much more rewarding.

"I'm just here to enjoy a festive New Year's Eve party, Mr. Peterson. No harm in that." I smiled angelically. "Now, if you'll excuse me, there are some people I would like to say hello to."

I started mingling, and people that I knew from the various campaigns I'd worked on began to approach me. I hardly needed to seek them out at all. They seemed genuinely happy to see me, and were excited that I was branching out on my own. One former client confided in me that they were not happy at all about the junior designer who had taken over my accounts.

Most of my former clients told me to contact them directly right after the holidays to set up a pitch. Inside, my nerves were rattling, and I could feel hysterical happiness bubbling up inside me. I looked around, wishing Kirin was here so that I could share my happiness with him. I knew how outlandish that thought was, but I was grateful that meeting him had been the catalyst I needed to move me in this direction.

I didn't want to dwell on that loss tonight. I stayed at the party a little while longer, leaving a short while before midnight.

As I left, I shook hands with many of my former—and soon to be new—business partners, hugging their spouses, and wishing them a happy New Year.

I walked confidently out of the ballroom, down the exquisite staircase, and through the elegant foyer of the hotel. Head held high, a smile in place, I walked out the double-doors into a New Year.

13

The rest of the winter flew by. I was so unbelievably busy after reaching out to my previous clients that I didn't have much time to think about Kirin. Now that I knew who he was, I had a heightened sense of awareness around an upcoming movie release, one that he had produced and starred in. It still boggled my mind that I'd hooked up with a major celebrity without even realizing who he was.

I'd opened a small office in the Maritime Building on Western Avenue, which was on the Seattle waterfront. I'd built out an open floor-plan so all the designers could collaborate together. I only had a team of six right now, but it was perfect, and the business was mine. I felt confident I could make this happen so quickly, and was excited about the journey ahead.

The clients made me work for their business. They weren't in the habit of changing design firms once they had established a relationship. Even though they knew me, I had to sell them on my vision for them, and where I could take them with their target-market needs.

In March, I got an email from Shaye inviting me to a spring fling party that she and her husband were hosting on the island. If I was open to it, she would arrange for me to fly up with Kenmore Air, a float plane service that flew out of Lake Union. It was also where she had worked for almost nine years.

The party was on the Saturday after the spring equinox, and she made reservations for me to fly up the Friday before. I'd been working hard these past few months, and really needed a short break. I was also looking forward to actually seeing Shaye, and thanking her for letting me stay over the holidays.

"Don't be late," she told me. "That's the last flight of the day."

I left work early that day, driving through the busy streets of Seattle to the south end of Lake Union.

Parking in the small, paid parking lot adjacent to the float plane office, I grabbed my travel bag and my laptop from the trunk of my car, and went through the double doors into a plush, elegant waiting area.

A cheerful young girl, no more than twenty years old, stood at a customer service podium, and greeted me with a friendly smile. "Good afternoon, welcome to Kenmore Air. How can I help you today?"

I set my bags on the floor in front of the desk and smiled back. Opening my wallet, I pulled out my driver's license and handed it to her. "Hi, I'm Caitlyn Darling. I think I have a flight to Lopez this afternoon?"

She took my license, glanced at her reservation log, and then looked back up at me. "Yes, ma'am. We have you scheduled for the four o'clock flight. If you could just place your bags here on the scale, we'll get you all set up."

I lifted both of my bags onto the silver scale and saw that it read 27.4.

Shaye had told me they had a twenty-five-pound luggage limit per person, so I needed to pack light. I looked back at the girl worriedly, but she smiled and waved me off. "There are just two of you today. I think we'll be fine."

She handed my license back to me, and I slid it back into my wallet.

"The pilot will be up to get you shortly. There is coffee over by the back wall, and you can wait inside or out on the deck. It's a nice view of the boats and planes from out there, and you'll hear Chris, the pilot, call you on the outside speakers."

She was so friendly. I would make sure I told Shaye how pleasant she was. "Thank you, but I think I'll stay in here."

I took a seat in the lobby and waited with a few other people that I assumed were flying to the other islands for the weekend. A man and his two kids were sitting together, and a woman who appeared disinterested, yet fashionable in her designer suit, was two seats away from them.

Sitting off by himself by a book rack was another man—a hippie type, with long greasy-looking gray hair and a beard. He looked scraggly and quite disgusting. In his baseball cap, Birkenstocks, tan cargo pants, and colorful Baja-style hoodie, I imagined that he was sitting far away because he most likely smelled. I felt a moment of guilt for judging him, but he did look very unkempt.

I sat down in one of the soft leather chairs and stared out at the water. It was so peaceful here, looking out at the planes all lined up along the dock, and the boats moored in the bay.

A young pilot dressed in white shorts and a blue zip up jacket with the Kenmore logo came into the office a short while later and called my name over the intercom system. "Flight to Lopez for Darling and Reid."

The name struck me as odd, but I was distracted when I noticed movement on the other side of the waiting area. The grungy guy stood and put on a pair of sunglasses, making his way to the door. Oh dear Lord, this was the other passenger.   Was he a relative of Shaye's? Maybe his first name was Reed, not his last name. I wasn't going to find out. I didn't want to talk to him.

I picked up my tote, and the hippie waited for me to reach the door. I held my breath as I walked by, hoping he wouldn't smell.

I followed the pilot out onto the dock, the dirty guy a few steps behind me, and when we reached the small yellow and white plane, the pilot stepped onto the pontoon and opened the back door.

"If you could just hand me your bags, I'll secure them in the back." He was perched up on a step, and I handed him my bag, watching as he took it and the hippie's back-pack and put them behind a mesh cargo net.

"One of you can ride up front if you'd like." He got off the step, stood on the pontoon, and held the door open for me as I got in.

"That's ok, I'll just sit back here." I said to him, hoping the hippie would climb up front.

Instead, he stepped in next to me, and the pilot shut the door behind him. I took a tentative sniff, pretending that I had a runny nose, and discovered that he didn't smell bad after all. He smelled kind of clean, like laundry detergent and fresh spring air.

Staring out at the water through the window, I scooted as close as I could to the inside wall of the plane, buckled up, and put the orange ear plugs in my ears to help damp the sound of the turbine engine.

The pilot climbed in to the front of the plane, and we started taxiing out into the bay, bouncing over the water like a power boat. I finally started to relax, and once we were up in the air, I could enjoy the view of the neighborhoods of Seattle. We followed the water from the lake over the locks, and out into Puget Sound towards the islands.

We didn't fly very high off the water, and I could see wake from the boats below us.

The man next to me was leaning against the window, and he appeared to be asleep. I glanced down at his body and saw that he wasn't a fat hippy. His thighs looked strong, and as I glanced down at his toes, I thought how unusual it was that someone who looked so slovenly had such well-manicured toenails.

After about an hour, the plane started its descent into Fisherman Bay, and I started to tear up. Maybe this was a mistake.

The hippy next to me rolled his head up, looked at me with his dark sunglasses on, and said in a smoker's voice, "Visiting friends?"

I turned and looked at him contemptuously. I really didn't want to engage in conversation with him. The engines were so loud, I pointed to my ears and mouthed, 'I can't hear you.' I thought I saw him smile before he turned back to look out his window.

The plane was flying lower over the water, and we bounced around a bit from the choppy air. I'd never landed on water before, so I didn't know what to expect. It was a little scary. I put my left hand on the seat next to me, and my right hand braced on the seat in front of me. When the plane dropped a bit, I caught my breath, and I thought I saw the guy next to me start to reach for me before the plane recovered, and we slowly started skimming on the water.

When the plane finally slowed and approached the dock, the pilot turned the engine off, and we drifted towards the dock. A teenage boy in khaki shorts and a polo shirt grabbed the ropes at the end of the wings and pulled the plane closer.

The pilot got out of the plane and opened the back door for us. I'd started thinking of my flying companion as 'Grungy Guy,' and I watched as he got out first, and then I followed him, slowly lowering myself down the steps to the pontoon and onto the dock. Both of us waited for the pilot to hand us our bags.

Grungy Guy took his bag and walked up the long dock to the resort at a clipped pace, disappearing inside before I was even halfway up the dock.

I walked up onto the deck outside the resort, opened a back door, and walked through the lobby to a gravel parking lot along the main bay road. I recognized the place now, although it had been closed when I was here over Christmas.

Shaye said she would send someone to get me, and I glanced back and forth on the road, looking for a car to arrive.

"Caitlyn Darling?" Oh no, no, no, no, no. I heard the smoker's voice behind me, and turned to see Grungy Guy.

Sheepishly, I asked, "Are you my ride?"

"I am."

I was praying this wasn't her husband. Shaye was classy and elegant, and I'd always imagined Nick as someone a lot more...normal. I remembered that he was a lawyer, so this wasn't connecting in my brain. "Are you Shaye's husband?"

"No."

Oh, thank God! "Relative?"

"Something like that."

He grabbed my bag, dismissed me, and proceeded to walk towards an old Ford truck.

I called after him, "Can you just give me a minute? I need to use the ladies' room."

He stopped and turned, took a moment to just look at me, and then continued on his way to the truck.

Making my way back into the resort lobby, I hid behind a fake plant and dialed Shaye's number. "Shaye, pick up, pick up, pick up." No answer. I sent a quick text asking if Grungy Guy was supposed to give me a ride. I waited for her response, anxiously watching the front door.

She finally responded, *yes, he's harmless*

Taking a deep breath, I pulled myself together, straightened my shoulders, and walked back out to the parking lot. He had pulled the truck up front, and left it idling as he jumped out of the driver's side to run around and open the door for me.

I narrowed my eyes as I glanced from the front of the truck to the bed, realizing that it looked familiar to me.

I asked Grungy Guy, "Is this your truck?"

"No."

As I moved toward it, I realized that this was the same truck the douchebag assistant from Los Angeles had been driving. Tentatively stepping into the car, I left one leg out, and Grungy Guy paused, waiting for me. Something about his mannerisms struck me as odd. They were too fluid, too graceful, and I looked a little closer at him. He lowered his eyes, and started shutting the door, forcing me to lift my leg.

He settled himself back into the driver's side and proceeded to pull the truck out onto the main bay road. I relaxed a little and enjoyed the scenic drive. The springtime flowers were starting to bloom alongside the road, and the trees had filled out with lush leaves. The ground was no longer covered in snow, and the fields were filled with hay.

Grungy Guy followed the bay road up a steep hill, and we ended up driving down the main road of the island.

Turning to him I said, "I've never been to Shaye's house. Do you know where we're going?"

He nodded and continued looking straight ahead. He propped his elbow up on the window ledge and spread his legs, relaxing into the drive. Something was oddly familiar about him, and I looked a little closer at him. He arms, his hands, the well-manicured toes…

Suddenly, I reached across the cab of the truck and yanked hard on his beard. He screamed and momentarily jerked the truck into the other lane, recovering before another car came along.

"What the heck? What was that for?"

He looked at me, amused and I hung my head in shame. "I'm so sorry. I thought...never mind. I'm...you reminded me of someone, and I'm so sorry, I thought you were him."

I turned back to stare out the window, and laughter started bubbling up inside me until it came out almost hysterically.

"Who do I remind you of?"

My laughter subsided, turning to soft hiccups and crying. I whispered, "It doesn't matter."

I was embarrassed, and I thought that maybe my feelings for Kirin were still too close to the surface.

We drove in silence for a short while, and then he started up a hill that looked familiar to me. "Wait. Stop. This is where Shaye's rental house is, not her house."

"I was told to take you here." He kept driving, and I was confused.

His face softened, and I saw his cheeks start to crease in a smile. I looked more objectively at him, at his hair—that looked greasy, but at second glance wasn't. Something was off. I wanted to tug on his beard again, but that was creepy. I saw him tilt his head towards me, his eyes shaded by his sunglasses, and he continued to the driveway of the house, gunning the engine to make it up the drive.

He stopped in front of the house, and I turned completely in my seat towards him. I moved fast, quickly reaching out and grabbing his hair. I tugged harder than I had on his beard, and it actually came off, his dark head now visible. He took off his sunglasses, and there he was, green eyes laughing back at me.

"Are you kidding me?!" I shouted as I got out of the truck. "I am going to kill her."

14

Slamming the truck door, I grabbed my bag out of the bed of the truck, and stormed up the stairs to the back door. I went to turn the handle, expecting it to be unlocked, and came up short against the door.

I looked under the coke container, where the key had been before, found the key, and unlocked the back door.

Kirin had grabbed his bag out of the back of the truck, and slowly walked up the back steps behind me. I shut the door in his face, and I heard him chuckle, as he calmly reached for the handle, opened the door, and followed me quietly into the house.

Dropping my bag on the floor, I went into the living room and tried to call Shaye. It went directly to voicemail, so I sent off a text: *I'm so mad at you*

Kirin had followed me into the room, set his bag on the couch, and tossed the keys on the end table.

"Cat, please listen to me."

"I don't want to listen to you."

He smiled adoringly at me. "I need to get this beard off. It's starting to itch. Can you just give me a minute? I want to explain."

I didn't respond, and he walked towards the downstairs bathroom.

The keys to the truck glittered at me from the table, and I grabbed them, and my bag, and ran for the door. I wasn't fast enough. Kirin heard my commotion and came running out of the bathroom, grabbing me in a bear hug before I could get out the door. He turned me around, pushing me gently against the wall, his body flush along mine, and he pried the keys out of my fingers.

This was an oddly familiar situation, and I saw the grin begin to grow on his face. His chest was pressed against me, and I saw my breasts heave. His eyes glanced down briefly, and they sparkled with humor.

"Let me go." I tried to sound angry, but my body betrayed me, and it sounded more like longing.

He laughed at me.

"It's not funny."

"Please, Cat. I need to get this beard off, I need a drink, and I want to explain. Please." His last word was a whisper, and a plea.

"Fine." I shook him off, and watched as he went back to the bathroom.

I went into the kitchen, opened the fridge, found a bottle of champagne, a container of orange juice, and a bottle of Lopez Island Chardonnay.

Reaching into the cupboard for a wine glass, I opened the bottle of wine, and poured myself a glass. I gulped down half of the glass and then filled it back up. Taking my glass, I went into the living room and sat on the couch to wait for him.

I looked around at the room, flooded by all the memories of our brief, yet meaningful time together here. I felt simultaneously betrayed by Shaye, and grateful that she was trying to do something romantic for me.

An overwhelming sense of peace started to roll over me, and when Kirin stepped back into the room, I felt my heart squeeze, and I inhaled sharply.

He had taken off the awful Baja sweater and was wearing a long-sleeved Maroon 5 T-shirt. He looked like Island Kirin, not Movie Star Alex, and I felt myself softening towards him.

Sitting down on the couch next to me, he shifted uncomfortably, looking deeply into my eyes, gauging my mood.

It was all I could do not to reach out and touch his freshly-shaved cheeks. He had a few spots of glue on his face, and I did reach out to pull them off. "You have...you have glue on your face."

He smiled at me, waited until I'd pulled it off, and then reached for my glass of wine. He drank down half of what I had left. "Need a refill?"

He didn't wait for a response as he stood from the couch, took my glass to the kitchen, and came back with my refilled glass and the bottle.

Setting the bottle on the table in front of us, he sat back down on the couch, turned to me and said, "You are so beautiful. I have missed you so much."

"You are so full of it."

He laughed at me. "Please just listen to me, and don't say anything until I'm finished."

I settled in, raised my eyebrows expectantly, and waited for him to continue.

"I've been trying to reach you. It took me awhile, but I need you to understand how frightening that situation was. When you showed up here, I had no idea who you were. You could have been paparazzi or another stalker. I had no idea, and I *did* want you to leave. But then, when I figured out you really had no idea who I was, I realized I enjoyed your company. And you were so cute, and funny, and, yes, incredible sexy."

He situated himself a little closer to me, and I felt myself being drawn to him.

Continuing softly, he said, "After a couple of days, I didn't want to tell you. I wanted to be *me*. It was so refreshing to just be with you." He cleared his throat. "I was going to tell you that night when we got back from lunch. I wanted you to know."

"Didn't you know James was coming to get you?"

"I'd stopped reading my emails. I was completely absorbed in you...I had no idea he was arriving that day, or that they had found her. As soon as I saw him at the door, I knew you were going to be angry. But I had to go. I had to take care of business, and then with the movie coming out, it was just really bad timing. And then, so much time had passed, I didn't know if what we had was real, or if you'd even listen to me if I did find you. But the thing is, the longer I was without you, the more I realized I wasn't going to get you out of my mind. It had been real for me."

He had slowly moved closer to me, so that his arm was across the back of the couch, and he was softly pushing the hair off my forehead with his fingers, his eyes lovingly roaming over my face.

Whispering, he said, "I have been doing everything to get back to you. When Ethan called and told me about the party, I called Shaye and asked her to help me get you here. I'm sorry if I upset you. I just needed you to hear me, and I didn't know if you would listen after not hearing from me for so long."

"You do know this can be considered kidnapping." I sounded petulant.

"That's ok. I think the charges are less than stalking and attempted murder, so I'll take my chances." His tone was accepting.

"I'm still hurt," I pouted.

"But you won't be forever." He was sliding closer and reached around my side. His face was getting closer to mine, and he whispered, "Cat, I'm so sorry things went down the way they did, and I'm sorry if not telling you hurt you. But one thing I'm glad came out of it, is that I'm absolutely certain about us. Cat, I'm going to tell you something very important…and I need you to repeat it back to me."

I looked at him dubiously. "Ok."

"I love you."

"I am not going to repeat that."

"Yes, you are!" He pulled his head back and looked at me with wide eyes.

"I'm still mad."

"I love you!"

"No, you don't."

200

"But I'm rich." He looked hurt, and I laughed.

"So am I." He looked at me speculatively. "Okay, maybe I'm not."

"I'm super sexy."

I teased him, "Says the media."

He was leaning towards me again, enjoying this game. "My mom loves me."

"She has to."

He turned serious, and I felt myself caving towards him. He took my wine glass out of my hands and held both my cheeks in his. "Cat, I love you. I will do anything for you. I don't want to be without you ever again. Everything is better, more perfect, with you."

"What are you going to do if I say it back to you?"

"I'm going to kiss you, and then I'm going to take you upstairs, get you naked, and make love to you all weekend long." He was almost completely wrapped around me now, nuzzling my neck.

"Oh, well...In that case, I love you, too."

ONE YEAR LATER...

This was madness. We had moved our corporate headquarters to Laguna Beach six months ago, and my team and I were running around the office getting ready for the launch of a new client's advertising campaign.

Kirin and I'd gotten married on Lopez Island last summer. We didn't want to wait. It was a small, intimate affair, with just our families, and he'd had to return to California right away for a film project.

After the wedding, I turned the running of the Seattle office over to another designer, and I had absolute confidence in her ability to manage our Northwest accounts.

My assistant here in Laguna Beach was a quirky designer that Kirin had introduced me to. She had previously been a set designer, and wanted to get out of the industry. In both her designs and her clothes, she had a retro style. From her black bobbed hair with thick bangs, to the Mary Janes on her feet, her style was one-hundred-percent vintage.

I was reviewing a storyboard for another new account when I heard the phone ringing and ringing. I looked up to see my assistant sitting on the edge of her desk watching a surfing competition taking place out the window.

I rapped my knuckles on the glass window of the conference room to get her attention, and pointed at the phone when she looked over at me.

She stepped back around her desk, clicking the button on her headset, and finally answered the phone. "Darling Media Group, this is Holly, how may I help you?"

Playlist

Havana Brown & Kronic – "Bullet Blowz"

Tujamo feat. Taio Cruz – "Booty Bounce"

Nikki & Rich – "Cat and Mouse"

Maroon 5 – "What Lovers Do"

Selena Gomez – "The Heart Wants What it Wants"

Pink – "Beautiful Trauma"

Zendaya – "Shake Santa Shake"

Sam Hunt – "House Party"

Hailee Steinfeld – "Starving"

Descendants 2 – "What's my name?"

Sigala – "Sweet Lovin'"

Made in the USA
Columbia, SC
27 July 2019